Great Epectations

Charles Dickens

STERLING CHILDREN'S BOOKS
New York

An Imprint of Sterling Publishing Co., Inc.
1166 Avenue of the Americas
New York, NY 10036

ISBN 978-1-4549-3972-6

DISTRIBUTED IN CANADA BY STERLING PUBLISHING CO., INC.
C/O CANADIAN MANDA GROUP, 664 ANNETTE STREET
TORONTO, ONTARIO M6S 2C8, CANADA

FOR INFORMATION ABOUT CUSTOM EDITIONS, SPECIAL SALES, AND PREMIUM
AND CORPORATE PURCHASES, PLEASE CONTACT STERLING SPECIAL SALES AT
800-805-5489 OR SPECIALSALES@STERLINGPUBLISHING.COM.

MANUFACTURED IN CHINA

LOT #:
2 4 6 8 10 9 7 5 3 1
05/20

STERLINGPUBLISHING.COM

Great Expectations

Charles Dickens

ILLUSTRATED BY
PENKO GELEV

RETOLD BY
JACQUELINE MORLEY

STERLING CHILDREN'S BOOKS
New York

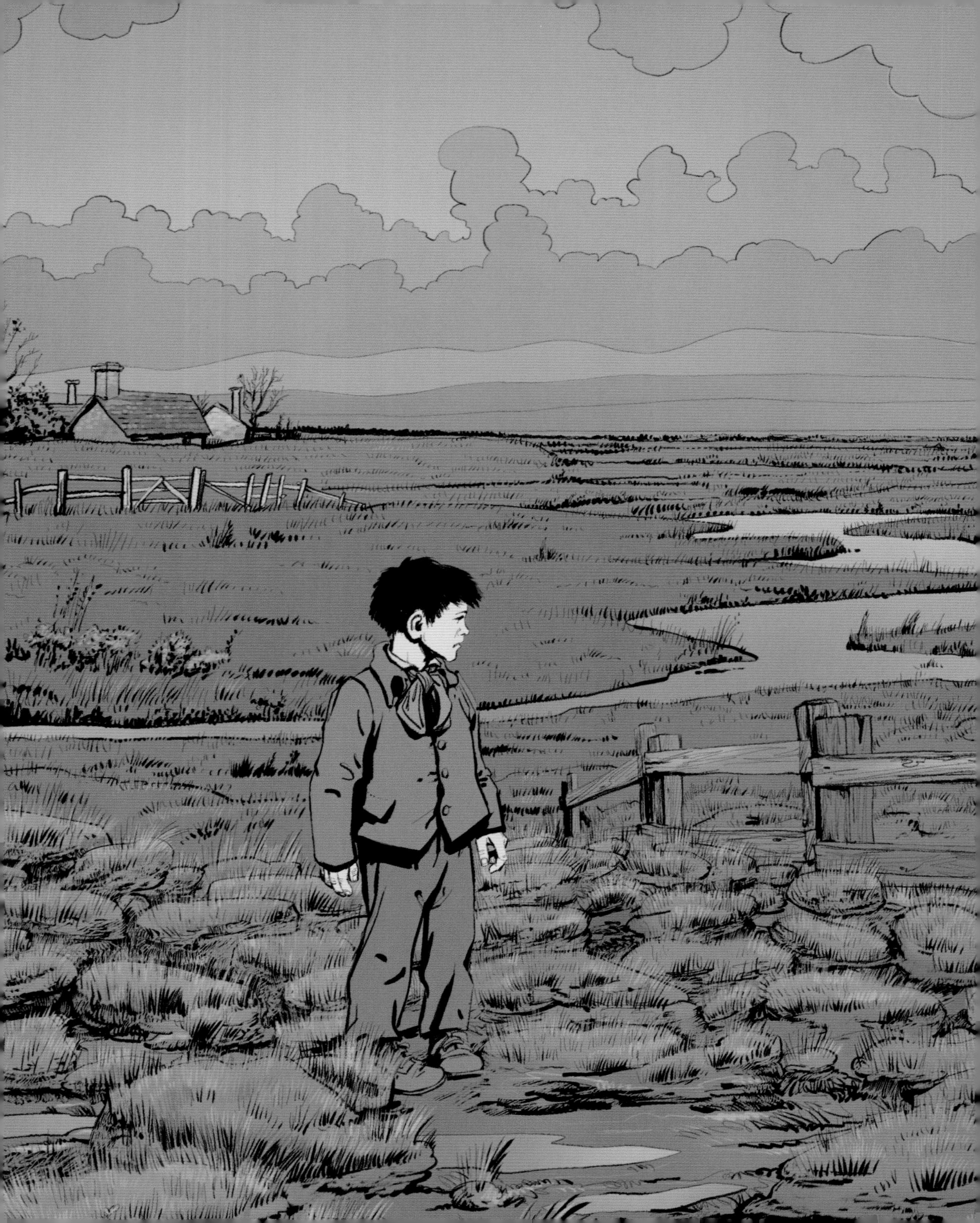

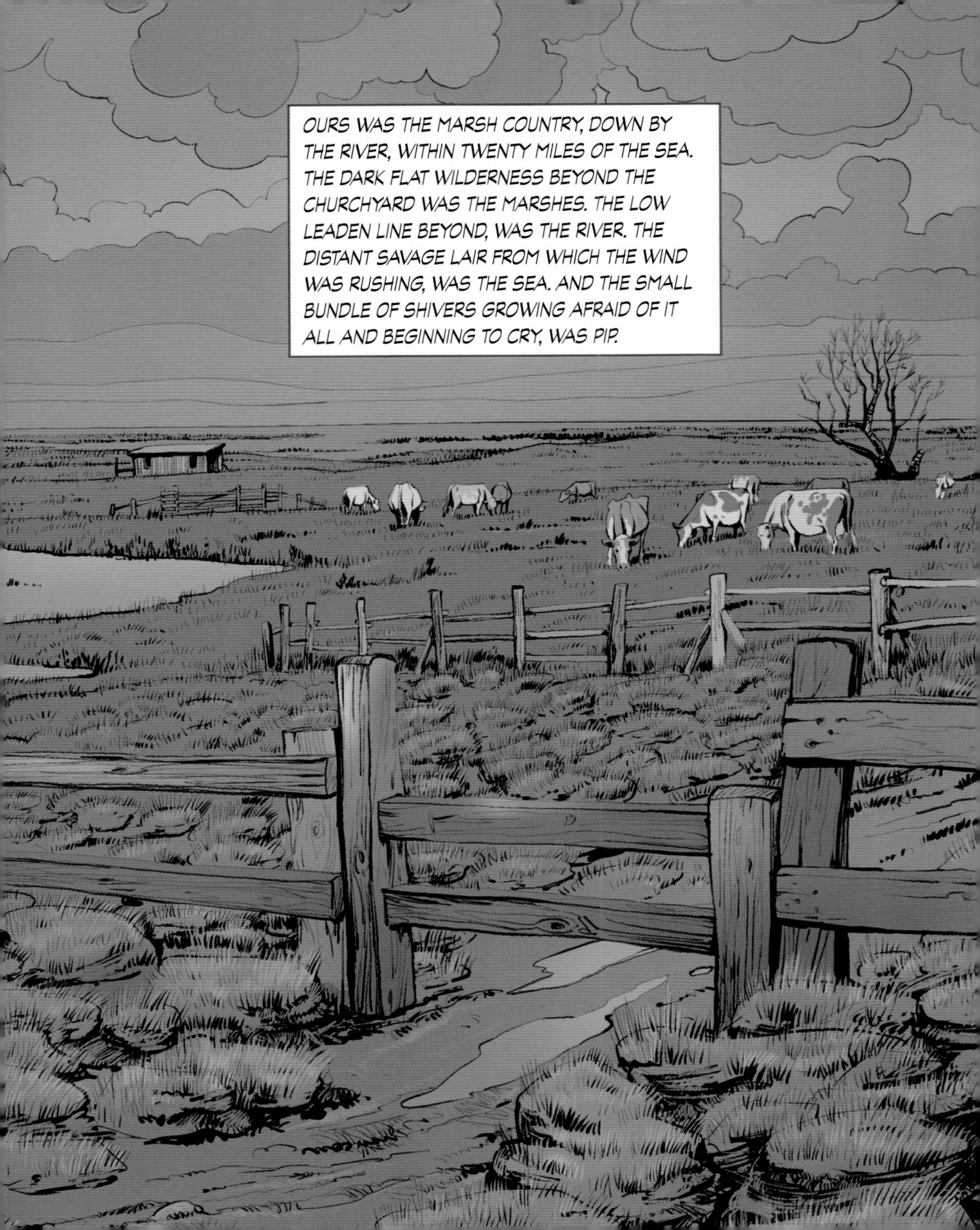
OURS WAS THE MARSH COUNTRY, DOWN BY THE RIVER, WITHIN TWENTY MILES OF THE SEA. THE DARK FLAT WILDERNESS BEYOND THE CHURCHYARD WAS THE MARSHES. THE LOW LEADEN LINE BEYOND, WAS THE RIVER. THE DISTANT SAVAGE LAIR FROM WHICH THE WIND WAS RUSHING, WAS THE SEA. AND THE SMALL BUNDLE OF SHIVERS GROWING AFRAID OF IT ALL AND BEGINNING TO CRY, WAS PIP.

CHARACTERS

PIP
AS A CHILD

PIP
AS A YOUNG MAN

MRS. JOE GARGERY,
PIP'S SISTER

JOE GARGERY,
BLACKSMITH,
PIP'S BROTHER-IN-LAW

ABEL MAGWITCH, A CONVICT

COMPEYSON,
MAGWITCH'S ENEMY

MR. PUMBLECHOOK,
JOE'S UNCLE

MISS HAVISHAM,
AN ELDERLY SPINSTER

ESTELLA, HER
ADOPTED DAUGHTER

BIDDY, A
VILLAGE GIRL

MR. JAGGERS,
A LONDON LAWYER

MOLLY, JAGGERS'S
HOUSEKEEPER

MR. WEMMICK,
JAGGERS'S CLERK

HERBERT POCKET,
A RELATIVE OF
MISS HAVISHAM

BENTLEY DRUMMLE,
A WEALTHY YOUNG MAN

ONE CHILLY CHRISTMAS EVE, A SMALL BOY STOOD AMONG THE TOMBSTONES IN A LONELY CHURCHYARD.

IT WAS A BLEAK, WINDSWEPT PLACE OVERLOOKING THE KENTISH[1] MARSHES THAT STRETCHED AWAY, FLAT AND SAD, TOWARD THE RIVER THAMES.[2]

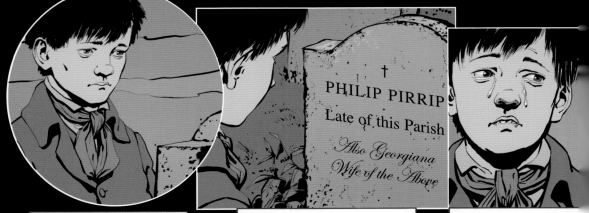

PHILIP PIRRIP
Late of this Parish
Also Georgiana
Wife of the Above

I WAS THAT SMALL BOY —NAMED PHILIP PIRRIP AFTER MY FATHER, BUT ALWAYS KNOWN AS PIP. THAT AFTERNOON WOULD SHAPE THE REST OF MY LIFE.

MY PARENTS DIED WHEN I WAS VERY YOUNG, SO I HAD NO MEMORY OF THEM. MY IDEA OF WHAT THEY WERE LIKE—SQUARE AND STIFF OR THIN AND CURLY—WAS TAKEN FROM THE LETTERING ON THEIR GRAVE.

THE SKY WAS DARKENING AND THE WIND ROSE. THE LONELINESS OF THE PLACE GREW SUDDENLY SO FRIGHTENING THAT I BEGAN TO CRY.

1. KENTISH: IN THE COUNTY OF KENT, IN THE SOUTHEAST CORNER OF ENGLAND. 2. THAMES: THE MAJOR RIVER THAT FLOWS THROUGH LONDON AND REACHES THE SEA BETWEEN THE COUNTIES OF KENT AND ESSEX.

JUST THEN . . .

1. FILE: A SHARP KNIFE-LIKE TOOL USED TO FILE DOWN METAL. 2 WITTLES: VICTUALS (FOOD). THE
CONVICT HAS A COCKNEY (WORKING CLASS LONDON) ACCENT.

A BOY MAY LOCK HIS DOOR, MAY BE WARM IN BED, MAY DRAW THE CLOTHES OVER HIS HEAD . . .

. . . BUT THAT YOUNG MAN WILL SOFTLY CREEP HIS WAY TO HIM AND TEAR HIM OPEN.

I PROMISED TO GET HIM A FILE AND ANY BITS OF FOOD I COULD.

SAY, LORD STRIKE YOU DEAD IF YOU DON'T!

LORD STRIKE ME DEAD IF I DON'T.

I WAS LATE GETTING HOME. JOE WARNED THAT MY SISTER WAS LOOKING FOR ME, IN A TERRIBLE TEMPER AS USUAL. ON HIS ADVICE I HID BEHIND THE KITCHEN DOOR.

WHERE HAVE YOU BEEN, YOU YOUNG MONKEY?

ONLY TO THE CHURCHYARD.

9

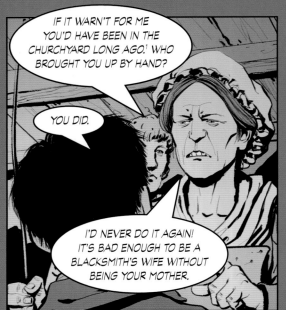

IF IT WARN'T FOR ME YOU'D HAVE BEEN IN THE CHURCHYARD LONG AGO.[1] WHO BROUGHT YOU UP BY HAND?

YOU DID.

I'D NEVER DO IT AGAIN! IT'S BAD ENOUGH TO BE A BLACKSMITH'S WIFE WITHOUT BEING YOUR MOTHER.

JOE AND I WERE EATING OUR SUPPER TOGETHER WHEN WE HEARD GUNFIRE.

CRACK!

WHAT DOES THAT MEAN, JOE?

THERE WAS A CONWICT OFF[2] LAST NIGHT. AND NOW, IT APPEARS, THEY'RE FIRING WARNING OF ANOTHER.

IT'S FROM THE HULKS.[3]

PEOPLE ARE PUT IN THE HULKS BECAUSE THEY MURDER AND ROB AND FORGE AND DO ALL SORTS OF BAD THINGS.

I DID NOT SLEEP FOR FEAR OF THE YOUNG MAN WHO MIGHT TEAR ME OPEN. AT DAWN I CREPT DOWNSTAIRS TO THE PANTRY.

A PORK PIE! PERHAPS IT WON'T BE MISSED.

1. YOU'D HAVE BEEN IN THE CHURCHYARD LONG AGO: YOU'D HAVE BEEN DEAD AND BURIED. 2. A CONWICT OFF: A CONVICT ESCAPED.
3. HULKS: SHIPS NO LONGER SEAWORTHY THAT WERE MOORED ON THE THAMES AND MEDWAY RIVERS TO SERVE AS PRISONS.

IT'S NOT HIM. IT MUST BE THE TERRIBLE YOUNG MAN!

MY CONVICT FELL ON THE FOOD LIKE A HUNGRY DOG.

WON'T YOU LEAVE ANY FOR THE YOUNG MAN? HE LOOKED VERY HUNGRY.

I'VE NO YOUNG MAN. WHO DID YOU SEE?

IT'S COMPEYSON! SHOW ME THE WAY HE WENT. I'LL PULL HIM DOWN LIKE A BLOODHOUND!

I THOUGHT IT WAS YOU AT FIRST. HE'S DRESSED LIKE YOU. HE HAD A BADLY BRUISED FACE.

NOT HERE?

YES, THERE!

HE BEGAN FILING HIS LEG-IRON LIKE A MADMAN, NOT MINDING HOW HE CUT INTO HIS LEG. I FLED.

BE GRATEFUL, BOY, TO THEM WHICH BROUGHT YOU UP BY HAND.

WHY IS IT THAT THE YOUNG ARE NEVER GRATEFUL?

JOE'S UNCLE PUMBLECHOOK, WHO WAS ALWAYS INVITED FOR CHRISTMAS, LECTURED ME AS USUAL, AND MADE THE CHRISTMAS MEAL MISERABLE FOR ME.

YOU MUST TASTE A DELICIOUS PRESENT OF UNCLE PUMBLECHOOK'S – A SAVORY PORK PIE.

MY CRIME WAS ABOUT TO BE DISCOVERED! I MADE A DASH FOR THE DOOR . . .

. . . AND RAN STRAIGHT INTO A ROW OF SOLDIERS ON THE DOORSTEP.

EXCUSE ME, LADIES AND GENTLEMEN. I WANT THE BLACKSMITH.

HOW FAR MIGHT YOU CALL YOURSELVES[2] FROM THE MARSHES?

JUST A MILE.

THEY WERE HUNTING TWO ESCAPED CONVICTS, AND NEEDED JOE TO MEND THEIR HANDCUFFS. THE PORK PIE WAS QUITE FORGOTTEN AS EVERYONE FOLLOWED JOE INTO THE FORGE.[1]

THAT'S NOT SO BAD. WE'LL CLOSE IN ON 'EM ABOUT DUSK.

JOE SUGGESTED THAT HE AND I GO DOWN WITH THE SOLDIERS AND SEE HOW THE HUNT WENT.

1. FORGE: A BLACKSMITH'S WORKSHOP. 2. HOW FAR MIGHT YOU CALL YOURSELVES?: HOW FAR DO YOU THINK YOU ARE?

IF YOU BRING THAT BOY BACK WITH HIS HEAD INJURED BY A MUSKET,[1] DON'T LOOK TO ME TO PUT IT BACK TOGETHER.

WE WENT UP AND DOWN BANKS, SPLASHED ACROSS DYKES[2] AND OVER THE OPEN MARSHES.

I SUPPOSE MY CONVICT THINKS IT'S ME THAT LED THE SOLDIERS HERE?

MURDERER!

CONVICTS! RUNAWAYS! GUARD! THIS WAY!

WE HEARD SHOUTS FROM A DISTANCE. THERE SEEMED TO BE TWO VOICES.

HERE ARE BOTH MEN! SURRENDER, YOU TWO!

I TOOK HIM! I GIVE HIM UP TO YOU! MIND[3] THAT!

1. MUSKET: A LONG-BARRELLED HANDGUN. 2: DYKES: WALLS MADE OF EARTH TO KEEP THE SEAWATER OFF THE LAND. 3. MIND: REMEMBER, TAKE NOTICE. PIP'S CONVICT HAS CAPTURED HIS ENEMY, INTENDING TO HAND HIM OVER TO THE SOLDIERS. HE IS DETERMINED THAT COMPEYSON MUST NOT GET AWAY EVEN THOUGH HE HIMSELF WILL BE CAPTURED AT THE SAME TIME.

THE SOLDIERS LIT TORCHES. IN THE SUDDEN LIGHT MY CONVICT SAW ME AND LOOKED AT ME HARD.

1. IT MAY . . . SUSPICION: HE DOESN'T WANT PIP TO BE BLAMED FOR STEALING THE FOOD.

YOU'RE WELCOME TO IT. WE WOULDN'T HAVE YOU STARVED TO DEATH, WOULD US, PIP?

AS THE CONVICTS WERE ROWED BACK TO THE HULK, MINE TURNED HIS HEAD AND LOOKED AT ME STILL.

THREE YEARS LATER . . .

NOW IF THIS BOY AN'T GRATEFUL THIS NIGHT, HE NEVER WILL BE!

MISS HAVISHAM WANTS THIS BOY TO GO AND PLAY CARDS AT HER HOUSE.

AND HE HAD BETTER PLAY THERE, OR I'LL WORK[1] HIM.

MISS HAVISHAM WAS AN IMMENSELY RICH AND GRIM LADY WHO NEVER LEFT HER HOUSE.

1. WORK: BEAT.

MISS HAVISHAM? I WONDER HOW SHE CAME TO KNOW PIP?

ISN'T IT JUST POSSIBLE, SEEING AS UNCLE PUMBLECHOOK IS HER TENANT,[1] SHE MIGHT ASK HIM IF HE KNEW OF A BOY TO GO AND PLAY THERE?

NOODLE! WHO SAID SHE KNEW HIM?

AND UNCLE PUMBLECHOOK, THINKING THIS BOY'S FORTUNE MAY BE MADE BY MISS HAVISHAM, HAS OFFERED TO TAKE HIM THERE.

LOR-A-MUSSY ME![2] GRIMED WITH SOOT AND DIRT FROM THE HAIR OF HIS HEAD TO THE SOLE OF HIS FOOT!

WHY ON EARTH AM I GOING TO PLAY AT MISS HAVISHAM'S?

TRUSSED UP TIGHT IN MY BEST SUIT, I WAS BUNDLED INTO UNCLE PUMBLECHOOK'S CHAISE-CART.[3]

1. TENANT: A PERSON WHO RENTS A HOUSE OR LAND OWNED BY ANOTHER PERSON. 2. LOR-A-MUSSY ME!: LORD HAVE MERCY ON ME. 3. CHAISE-CART: LIGHT TWO-WHEELED CARRIAGE.

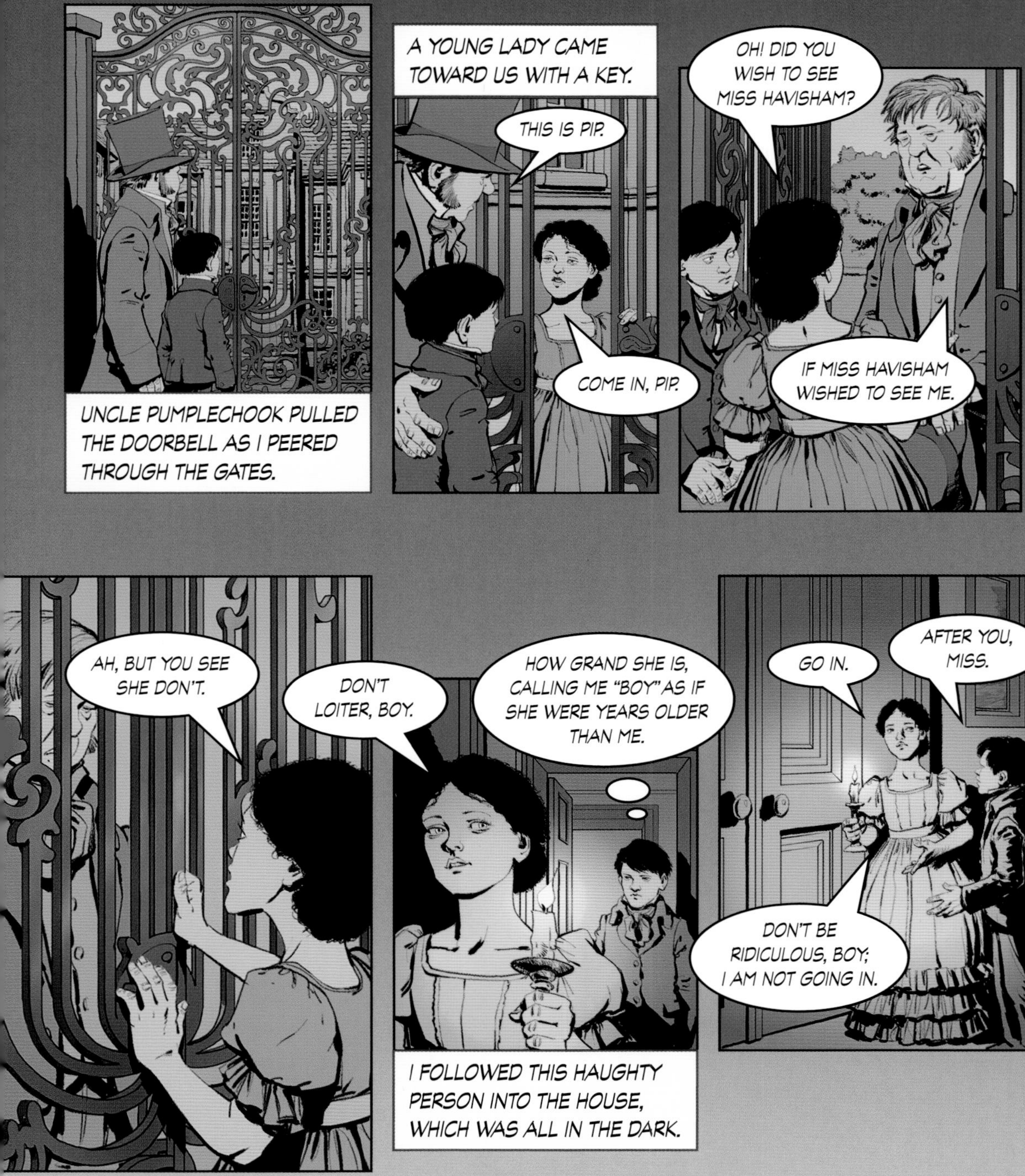

UNCLE PUMPLECHOOK PULLED THE DOORBELL AS I PEERED THROUGH THE GATES.
A YOUNG LADY CAME TOWARD US WITH A KEY.
THIS IS PIP.
COME IN, PIP.
OH! DID YOU WISH TO SEE MISS HAVISHAM?
IF MISS HAVISHAM WISHED TO SEE ME.
AH, BUT YOU SEE SHE DON'T.
DON'T LOITER, BOY.
HOW GRAND SHE IS, CALLING ME "BOY" AS IF SHE WERE YEARS OLDER THAN ME.
I FOLLOWED THIS HAUGHTY PERSON INTO THE HOUSE, WHICH WAS ALL IN THE DARK.
GO IN.
AFTER YOU, MISS.
DON'T BE RIDICULOUS, BOY; I AM NOT GOING IN.

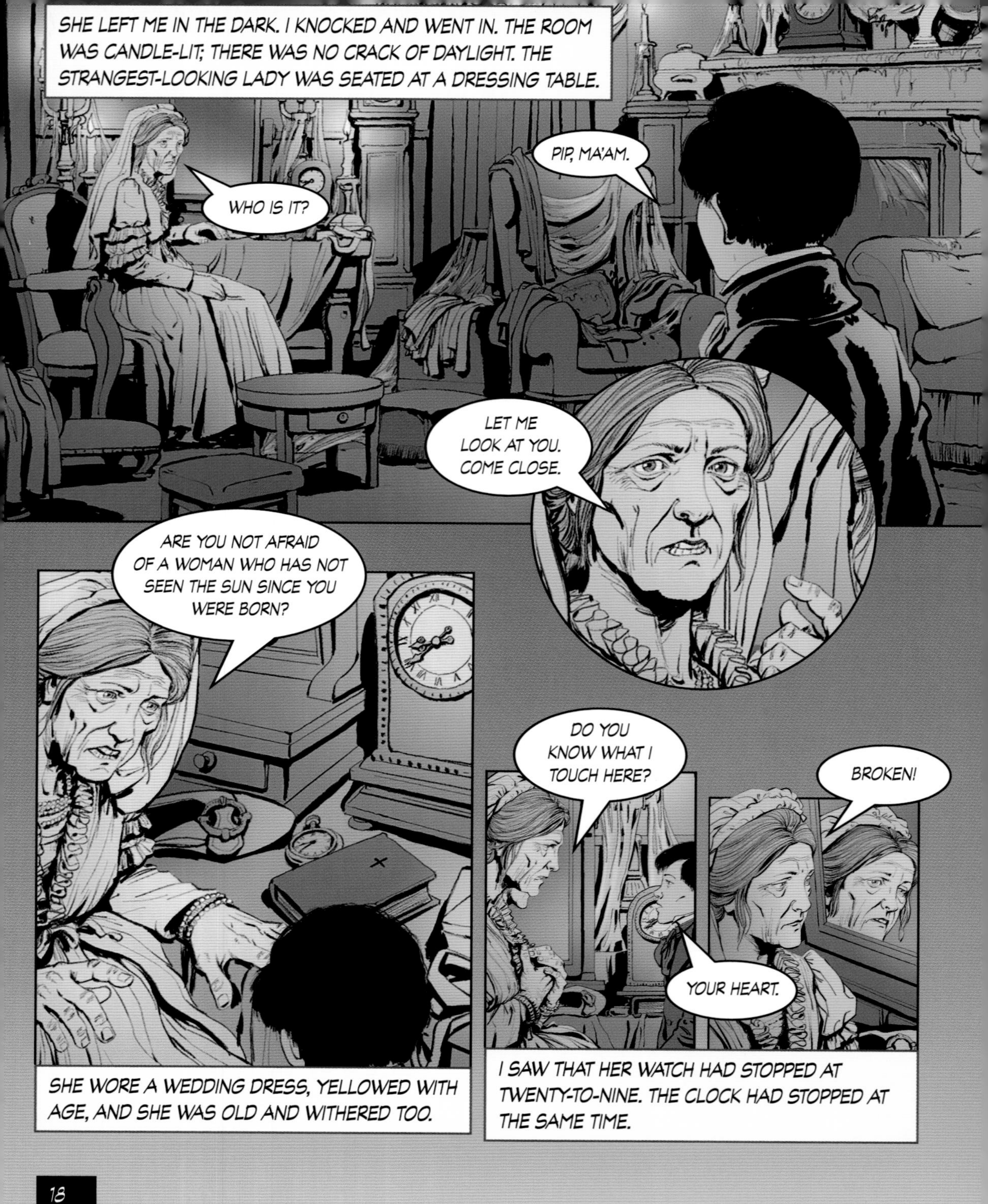
SHE LEFT ME IN THE DARK. I KNOCKED AND WENT IN. THE ROOM WAS CANDLE-LIT; THERE WAS NO CRACK OF DAYLIGHT. THE STRANGEST-LOOKING LADY WAS SEATED AT A DRESSING TABLE.
WHO IS IT?
PIP, MA'AM.
LET ME LOOK AT YOU. COME CLOSE.
ARE YOU NOT AFRAID OF A WOMAN WHO HAS NOT SEEN THE SUN SINCE YOU WERE BORN?
SHE WORE A WEDDING DRESS, YELLOWED WITH AGE, AND SHE WAS OLD AND WITHERED TOO.
DO YOU KNOW WHAT I TOUCH HERE?
YOUR HEART.
BROKEN!
I SAW THAT HER WATCH HAD STOPPED AT TWENTY-TO-NINE. THE CLOCK HAD STOPPED AT THE SAME TIME.

I AM TIRED. I HAVE A FANCY THAT I WANT[1] TO SEE SOMEONE PLAY.

PLAY, PLAY, PLAY!

ARE YOU SULLEN AND OBSTINATE?[2]

NO, MA'AM. I WOULD PLAY IF I COULD, BUT IT'S SO STRANGE HERE AND SO FINE...

CALL ESTELLA. AT THE DOOR. YOU CAN DO THAT.

LET ME SEE YOU PLAY CARDS WITH THIS BOY.

WITH THIS BOY! WHY, HE IS A COMMON LABORING[3] BOY!

1. I HAVE . . . I WANT: I WOULD LIKE. 2. SULLEN AND OBSTINATE: SULKY AND STUBBORN.
3. LABORING: WORKING-CLASS.

1. KNAVES: ANOTHER TERM FOR "JACKS" IN PLAYING CARDS.

20

ESTELLA BROUGHT ME SOMETHING TO EAT IN THE YARD, AS IF I WERE A DOG. WHILE SHE WAS GONE I HID MY FACE AND SOBBED.

I WENT HOME FEELING I WAS COARSE AND COMMON, AND THAT EVERYTHING ABOUT ME – MY HOME, THE FORGE, AND EVEN DEAR JOE – WAS COMMON, TOO.

NEXT WEEK BY APPOINTMENT I RETURNED TO MISS HAVISHAM'S.

I LIED. I WAS INWARDLY CRYING FOR HER THEN, AND IN THE FUTURE SHE WAS TO COST ME MUCH MORE PAIN.

ON THE STAIRS WE MET A BURLY GENTLEMAN WITH SHARP, SUSPICIOUS EYES. HIS HANDS SMELLED OF SCENTED SOAP. I HAD NO IDEA THEN OF THE PART HE WAS TO PLAY IN MY LIFE.

MISS HAVISHAM AND HER ROOM WERE JUST AS I HAD LEFT THEM.

I CROSSED THE LANDING AND OPENED THE DOOR. THE ROOM HAD ONCE BEEN VERY GRAND BUT EVERYTHING IN IT WAS COATED IN DUST AND BREAKING INTO PIECES. SOME SORT OF FEAST ROTTED ON THE TABLE.

THERE WAS A RATTLING OF MICE IN THE SKIRTING AND ALL SORTS OF CRAWLY THINGS WERE RUNNING ABOUT. SUDDENLY THERE WAS A HAND ON MY SHOULDER.

THIS IS WHERE I SHALL BE LAID WHEN I AM DEAD.

WHAT DO YOU THINK THAT IS?

I CAN'T GUESS WHAT IT IS, MA'AM.

IT'S A GREAT CAKE. A BRIDE-CAKE. MINE!

COME! WALK ME!

MY JOB WAS TO WALK HER AROUND AND AROUND, WHILE SHE GAZED AT THE ROTTING FEAST.

LATER, IN THE OVERGROWN GARDEN, I BUMPED INTO A PALE YOUNG GENTLEMAN OF MY OWN AGE.

WHO GAVE YOU LEAVE[1] TO PROWL ABOUT?

MISS ESTELLA.

COME AND FIGHT.

LAWS OF THE GAME! REGULAR RULES!

WHY IS HE DANCING ABOUT LIKE THAT? IS THAT HOW GENTLEMEN FIGHT?

1. LEAVE: PERMISSION.

23

I STRUCK THE FIRST BLOW. I WAS NEVER SO SURPRISED IN MY LIFE!

CRACK!

HE KEPT GETTING UP, AND I KEPT KNOCKING HIM DOWN. SOON HE WAS BRUISED ALL OVER. I HAD TO ADMIRE HIS SPIRIT.

YOU'VE WON. SHAKE HANDS.

CAN I HELP YOU?

NO, THANKEE.

YOU MAY KISS ME IF YOU LIKE.

SHE OFFERS IT LIKE A PIECE OF MONEY.[1] IT DOESN'T MEAN ANYTHING.

AFTER THIS I CAME REGULARLY TO MISS HAVISHAM'S.

BREAK THEIR HEARTS, MY PRIDE AND HOPE – BREAK THEIR HEARTS AND HAVE NO MERCY!

VERY MUCH, MA'AM.

DOES SHE GROW PRETTIER AND PRETTIER, PIP?

BUT ESTELLA NEVER LET ME KISS HER AGAIN.

I TOLD MISS HAVISHAM I WAS TO BE APPRENTICED[2] TO JOE.

LET GARGERY COME HERE WITH YOU, AND BRING YOUR INDENTURES.[3]

1. LIKE A PIECE OF MONEY: SHE LOOKS DOWN AT HIM, LIKE A RICH PERSON GIVING A COIN TO A BEGGAR. 2. APPRENTICED: BOUND BY A LEGAL AGREEMENT TO WORK FOR A CRAFTSMAN FOR A SPECIFIED TIME, TO LEARN HIS TRADE. 3. INDENTURES: THE CONTRACT BETWEEN A MASTER CRAFTSMAN AND HIS APPRENTICE.

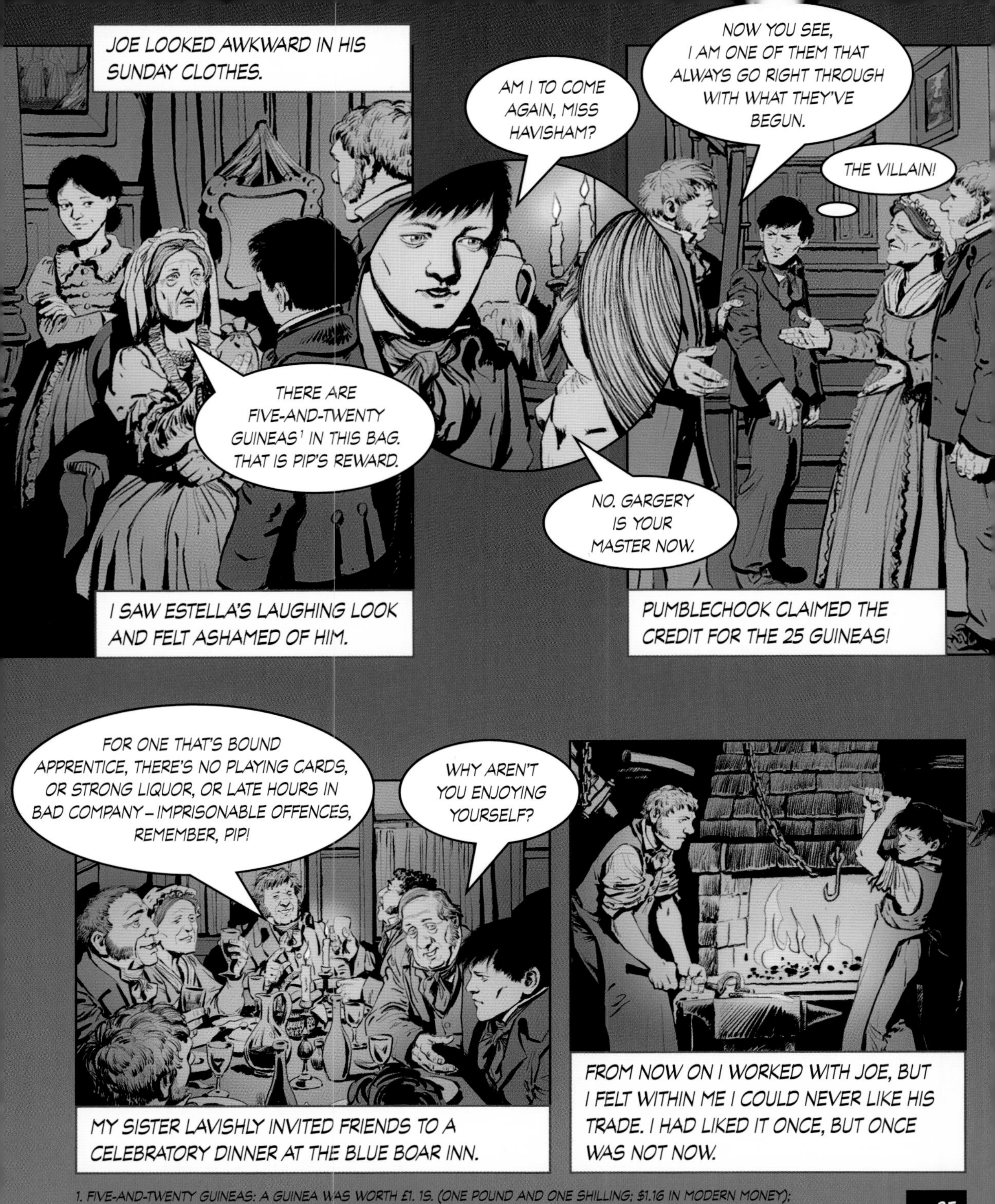
JOE LOOKED AWKWARD IN HIS SUNDAY CLOTHES.
AM I TO COME AGAIN, MISS HAVISHAM?
THERE ARE FIVE-AND-TWENTY GUINEAS[1] IN THIS BAG. THAT IS PIP'S REWARD.
NO. GARGERY IS YOUR MASTER NOW.
I SAW ESTELLA'S LAUGHING LOOK AND FELT ASHAMED OF HIM.
NOW YOU SEE, I AM ONE OF THEM THAT ALWAYS GO RIGHT THROUGH WITH WHAT THEY'VE BEGUN.
THE VILLAIN!
PUMBLECHOOK CLAIMED THE CREDIT FOR THE 25 GUINEAS!
FOR ONE THAT'S BOUND APPRENTICE, THERE'S NO PLAYING CARDS, OR STRONG LIQUOR, OR LATE HOURS IN BAD COMPANY – IMPRISONABLE OFFENCES, REMEMBER, PIP!
WHY AREN'T YOU ENJOYING YOURSELF?
MY SISTER LAVISHLY INVITED FRIENDS TO A CELEBRATORY DINNER AT THE BLUE BOAR INN.
FROM NOW ON I WORKED WITH JOE, BUT I FELT WITHIN ME I COULD NEVER LIKE HIS TRADE. I HAD LIKED IT ONCE, BUT ONCE WAS NOT NOW.

1. FIVE-AND-TWENTY GUINEAS: A GUINEA WAS WORTH £1. 1S. (ONE POUND AND ONE SHILLING; $1.16 IN MODERN MONEY); 25 GUINEAS IS $29.05. THIS IS A GENEROUS GIFT TO PAY FOR PIP'S APPRENTICESHIP.

SOON AFTER THIS, MY SISTER SUFFERED A DREADFUL HEAD INJURY. BIDDY, A KINDLY VILLAGE GIRL, CAME TO CARE FOR HER. I FELT I COULD CONFIDE IN BIDDY.

I WANT TO BE A GENTLEMAN.

DON'T YOU THINK YOU'RE HAPPIER AS YOU ARE?

BIDDY, I AM DISGUSTED WITH MY CALLING[1] AND MY LIFE. I WOULDN'T MIND BEING SO COARSE AND COMMON, IF NOBODY HAD TOLD ME SO!

IT WAS NEITHER A VERY TRUE NOR A VERY POLITE THING TO SAY. WHO SAID IT?

THE BEAUTIFUL YOUNG LADY AT MISS HAVISHAM'S. I ADMIRE HER DREADFULLY, AND I WANT TO BE A GENTLEMAN ON HER ACCOUNT.

TO SPITE HER OR TO GAIN HER OVER?

I DON'T KNOW.

1. MY CALLING: MY TRADE.

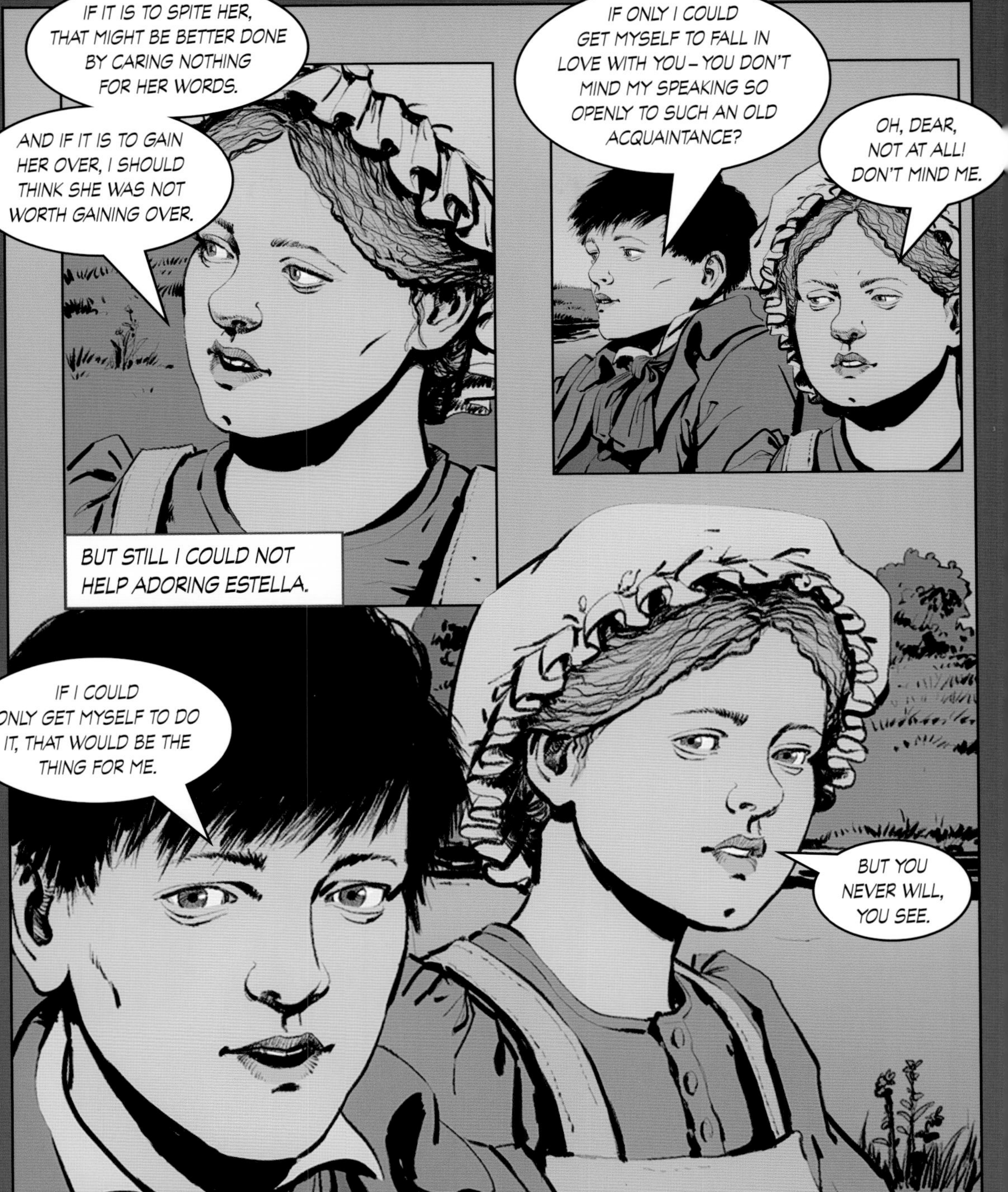
IF IT IS TO SPITE HER, THAT MIGHT BE BETTER DONE BY CARING NOTHING FOR HER WORDS.
AND IF IT IS TO GAIN HER OVER, I SHOULD THINK SHE WAS NOT WORTH GAINING OVER.
BUT STILL I COULD NOT HELP ADORING ESTELLA.
IF ONLY I COULD GET MYSELF TO FALL IN LOVE WITH YOU – YOU DON'T MIND MY SPEAKING SO OPENLY TO SUCH AN OLD ACQUAINTANCE?
OH, DEAR, NOT AT ALL! DON'T MIND ME.
IF I COULD ONLY GET MYSELF TO DO IT, THAT WOULD BE THE THING FOR ME.
BUT YOU NEVER WILL, YOU SEE.

IN THE FOURTH YEAR OF MY APPRENTICESHIP I RECEIVED AN UNEXPECTED VISITOR.

I AM HERE.

JOSEPH GARGERY? YOU HAVE AN APPRENTICE, COMMONLY KNOWN AS PIP? IS HE HERE?

MY NAME IS JAGGERS, AND I AM A LAWYER FROM LONDON. I HAVE UNUSUAL BUSINESS WITH YOU.

HE'S THE MAN WE MET ON THE STAIRS AT MISS HAVISHAM'S!

NOW, JOSEPH GARGERY, I AM THE BEARER OF AN OFFER[1] TO RELIEVE YOU OF YOUR APPRENTICE.

MY DREAM IS REALITY!

HE WILL COME INTO A HANDSOME PROPERTY.[2] HE IS TO BE BROUGHT UP AS A GENTLEMAN – IN A WORD, AS A YOUNG FELLOW OF GREAT EXPECTATIONS.[3]

I AM THE BEARER OF AN OFFER: I HAVE COME TO TELL YOU ABOUT AN OFFER (MADE BY SOMEONE ELSE).
A HANDSOME PROPERTY: A GENEROUS AMOUNT OF MONEY.
A YOUNG FELLOW OF GREAT EXPECTATIONS: A YOUNG MAN WHO IS EXPECTED TO BE VERY SUCCESSFUL IN LIFE.

YOU ARE TO UNDERSTAND, MR. PIP, THAT THE NAME OF YOUR BENEFACTOR[1] REMAINS A PROFOUND SECRET UNTIL THAT PERSON CHOOSES TO REVEAL IT.

WHEN THAT MAY BE, I CANNOT SAY. YOU ARE PROHIBITED FROM MAKING ANY INQUIRY ON THIS MATTER.

MISS HAVISHAM IS GOING TO MAKE MY FORTUNE!

MY HEART WAS BEATING SO FAST THAT I COULD BARELY SPEAK.

YOU SHOULD HAVE SOME NEW CLOTHES. SHALL I LEAVE YOU TWENTY GUINEAS?

I WAS TO STUDY IN LONDON WITH MR. MATTHEW POCKET. I KNEW THAT NAME—HE WAS A RELATION OF MISS HAVISHAM'S!

I HAVE COME INTO SUCH GOOD FORTUNE, MISS HAVISHAM, AND I AM SO GRATEFUL FOR IT.

BE GOOD—DESERVE IT—ABIDE BY MR. JAGGERS'S INSTRUCTIONS.

I SAID FAREWELL TO MY FAIRY GODMOTHER. REMEMBERING JAGGERS'S WARNING, I DID NOT OPENLY THANK HER.

1. YOUR BENEFACTOR: THE PERSON WHO IS BEING GENEROUS TO YOU.

GOODBYE, MY DEAR, DEAR FRIEND!

JOE WANTED TO WALK ME TO THE COACH, BUT I THOUGHT IT WOULD SPOIL MY NEW LOOK.

YOU'RE THE PROWLING BOY!

AND YOU ARE THE PALE YOUNG GENTLEMAN!

I WAS TO SHARE CHAMBERS[1] IN LONDON WITH MY TUTOR'S SON, HERBERT POCKET. I MET HIM ON THE STAIRS.

I HOPE YOU'LL FORGIVE ME FOR HAVING KNOCKED YOU ABOUT SO.

THAT'S NOT QUITE HOW I REMEMBER IT!

I HEAR YOU'VE COME INTO GOOD FORTUNE.

MISS HAVISHAM SENT FOR ME ONCE. PERHAPS I SHOULD HAVE BEEN ENGAGED TO ESTELLA!

1. CHAMBERS: RENTED ROOMS.

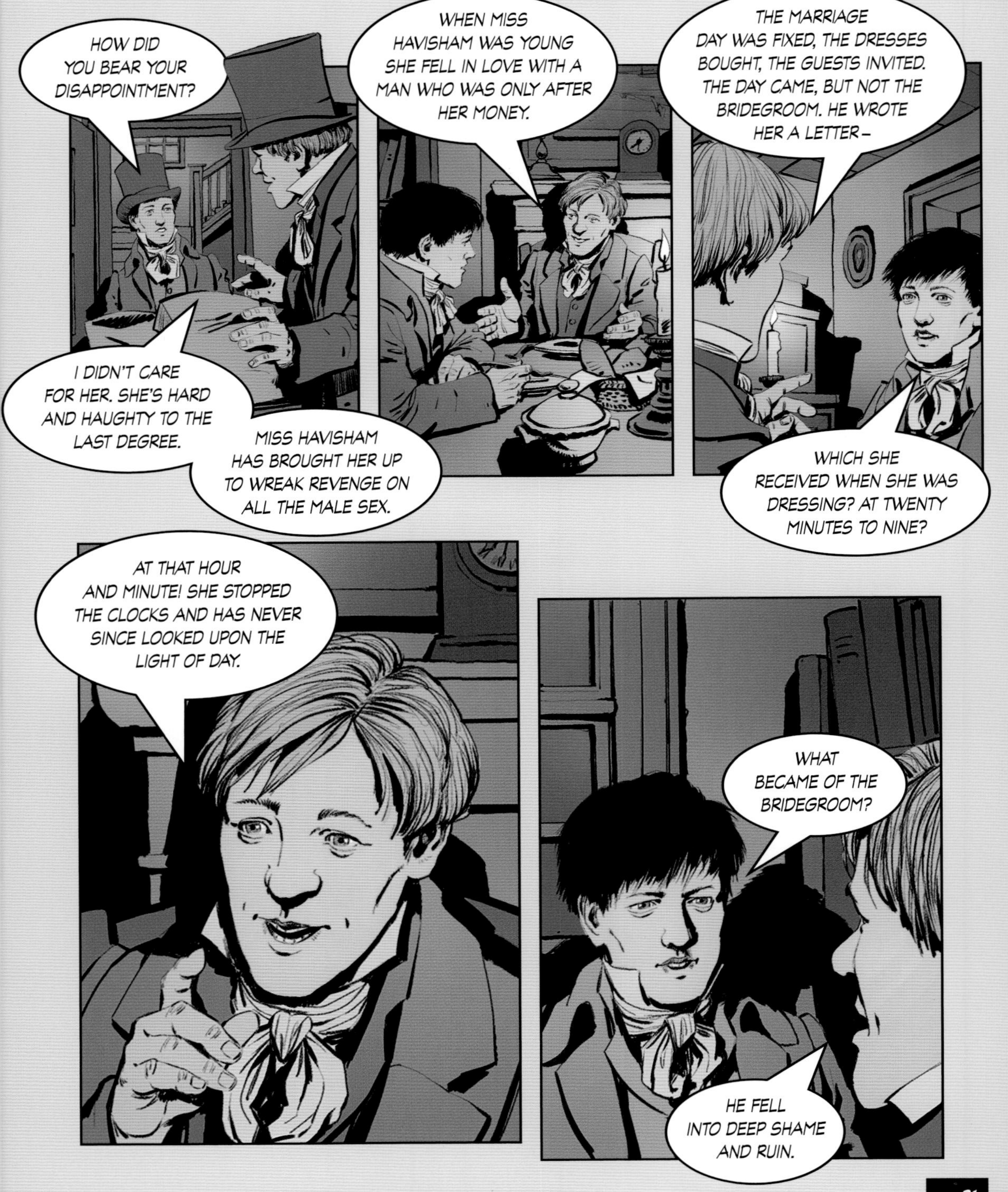
HOW DID YOU BEAR YOUR DISAPPOINTMENT?
I DIDN'T CARE FOR HER. SHE'S HARD AND HAUGHTY TO THE LAST DEGREE.
MISS HAVISHAM HAS BROUGHT HER UP TO WREAK REVENGE ON ALL THE MALE SEX.
WHEN MISS HAVISHAM WAS YOUNG SHE FELL IN LOVE WITH A MAN WHO WAS ONLY AFTER HER MONEY.
THE MARRIAGE DAY WAS FIXED, THE DRESSES BOUGHT, THE GUESTS INVITED. THE DAY CAME, BUT NOT THE BRIDEGROOM. HE WROTE HER A LETTER–
WHICH SHE RECEIVED WHEN SHE WAS DRESSING? AT TWENTY MINUTES TO NINE?
AT THAT HOUR AND MINUTE! SHE STOPPED THE CLOCKS AND HAS NEVER SINCE LOOKED UPON THE LIGHT OF DAY.
WHAT BECAME OF THE BRIDEGROOM?
HE FELL INTO DEEP SHAME AND RUIN.

HERBERT WORKED IN SHIPPING INSURANCE.

ARE THE PROFITS LARGE?

WHY, N-NO: NOT TO ME.

THAT IS, IT DOESN'T PAY ME ANYTHING . . .

I FEARED HE WOULD NEVER BE A GREAT BUSINESSMAN.

YOU'LL FALL IN THE RIVER AND BE DROWNDED,[1] AND WHAT'LL YOUR PA SAY THEN!

THE POCKETS WERE NOT WELL OFF. FOUR SMALL POCKETS RACED ABOUT THE GARDEN, BUT MRS. POCKET FANCIED HERSELF TOO GRAND A LADY TO BOTHER WHAT THEY DID.

I'M NEXT HEIR BUT ONE TO THE BARONETCY,[2] YOU KNOW.

HERBERT'S FATHER HAD A SECOND STUDENT, CALLED BENTLEY DRUMMLE. HE WAS SULKY, AND A WORSE SNOB THAN MRS. POCKET.

1. DROWNDED: A MISPRONUNCIATION OF "DROWNED." 2. BARONETCY: THE RANK OF BARONET (ABOVE A KNIGHT BUT BELOW A BARON).

MR. JAGGERS OFTEN SPOKE HARSHLY TO ME. HIS CLERK, WEMMICK, TOLD ME NOT TO MIND ABOUT IT.

I HARDLY KNOW WHAT TO MAKE OF MR. JAGGERS'S MANNER.

HE DON'T MEAN YOU SHOULD KNOW. HE'S DEEP — DEEP AS AUSTRALIA.

IF YOU'D CARE TO VISIT ME AT HOME, I SHOULD CONSIDER IT AN HONOR.

I SHOULD BE DELIGHTED.

WELL. AT LEAST HE'S HUMAN.

THANKEE. HAVE YOU DINED WITH MR. JAGGERS YET?

NOT YET.

WHEN YOU DO — LOOK AT HIS HOUSEKEEPER.

YOU'LL SEE A WILD BEAST TAMED. IT WON'T LOWER YOUR OPINION OF MR. JAGGERS'S POWERS.

MR. JAGGERS'S DINNER INVITATION INCLUDED HERBERT AND BENTLEY DRUMMLE.

BENTLEY DRUMMLE? I LIKE THE LOOK OF THAT FELLOW.

THE HOUSEKEEPER WAS VERY PALE, WITH LARGE, FADED EYES WHICH SHE KEPT FIXED ON JAGGERS.

CONCEIT OAF.

I COULD SCATTER YOU ALL LIKE CHAFF.[1]

THE TALK TURNED TO ROWING. DRUMMLE STARTED BOASTING OF HIS MUSCLE POWER.

1. LIKE CHAFF: LIKE SOMETHING VERY LIGHT AND WORTHLESS (CHAFF IS THE BITS LEFT OVER FROM GRAIN AFTER IT

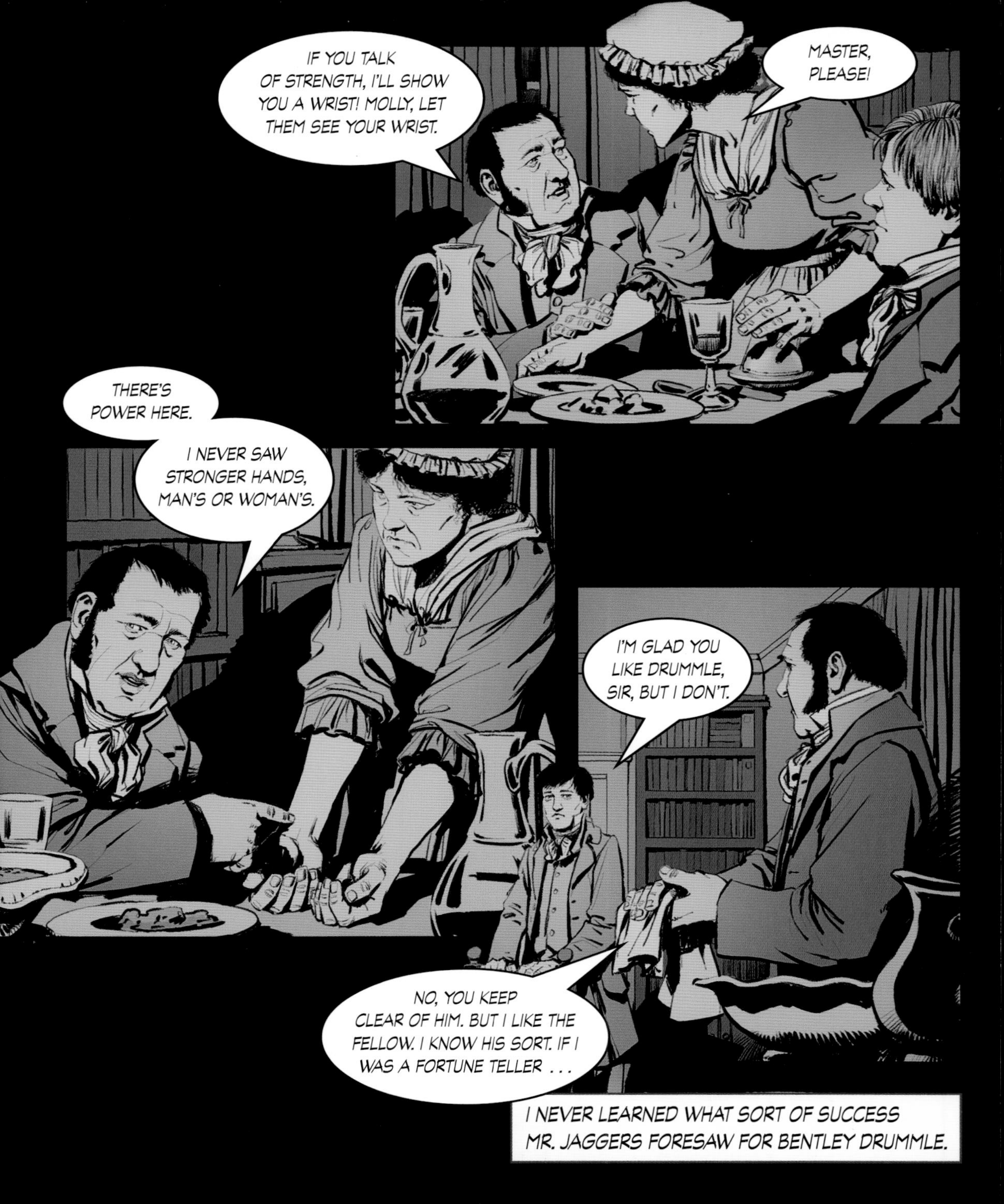
IF YOU TALK OF STRENGTH, I'LL SHOW YOU A WRIST! MOLLY, LET THEM SEE YOUR WRIST.
MASTER, PLEASE!
THERE'S POWER HERE.
I NEVER SAW STRONGER HANDS, MAN'S OR WOMAN'S.
I'M GLAD YOU LIKE DRUMMLE, SIR, BUT I DON'T.
NO, YOU KEEP CLEAR OF HIM. BUT I LIKE THE FELLOW. I KNOW HIS SORT. IF I WAS A FORTUNE TELLER . . .
I NEVER LEARNED WHAT SORT OF SUCCESS MR. JAGGERS FORESAW FOR BENTLEY DRUMMLE.

A LETTER FROM BIDDY . . .

JOE IS COMING TO VISIT! WHAT WILL MY FRIENDS MAKE OF HIM?

PIP! YOU HAVE THAT GROWED AND THAT SWELLED AND THAT GENTLEFOLKED! [1]

NOW THAT I LIVED LIKE A FINE GENTLEMAN, I WOULD GLADLY HAVE PAID TO KEEP HIM AWAY.

I AM GLAD TO SEE YOU, JOE.

NOT KNOWING WHAT TO DO WITH HIS HAT, HE STUCK IT ON THE MANTELPIECE, WHERE IT KEPT FALLING OFF.

THE VISIT WAS NOT A SUCCESS. JOE STARTED CALLING ME "SIR." EVEN HERBERT COULD NOT PUT HIM AT HIS EASE. I HAD NOT THE SENSE TO SEE THAT IT WAS MY FAULT.

TEA OR COFFEE, MR. GARGERY?

THANKEE, SIR. I'LL TAKE WHICHEVER IS MOST AGREEABLE TO YOURSELF.

1. YOU . . . GENTLEFOLKED: YOU HAVE GROWN UP, FILLED OUT, AND BECOME A GENTLEMAN.

JOE BROUGHT A MESSAGE FROM MISS HAVISHAM: ESTELLA WAS BACK FROM ABROAD AND WOULD LIKE TO SEE ME.

BIDDY, WHEN I ASKED HER TO WRITE IT TO YOU, SHE SAYS, "HE WILL BE GLAD TO HAVE IT BY WORD OF MOUTH. YOU WANT TO SEE HIM – GO!"

I HAVE NOW CONCLUDED, SIR, AND, PIP, I WISH YOU EVER PROSPERING.

BUT YOU ARE NOT GOING NOW, JOE?

PIP, OLD CHAP, YOU AND ME IS NOT TWO FIGURES TO BE TOGETHER IN LONDON.

THINK OF ME IN MY FORGE, WITH MY HAMMER IN MY HAND.

GOD BLESS YOU, DEAR OLD PIP, OLD CHAP, GOD BLESS YOU.

I WAS SHAMED BY HIS SIMPLE DIGNITY. I RAN AFTER HIM INTO THE STREET, BUT HE WAS GONE.

I WENT TO SEE MISS HAVISHAM THE NEXT DAY. AT FIRST I DID NOT RECOGNISE THE ELEGANT LADY NEXT TO HER.

HAS HE CHANGED?

THAT WAS LONG AGO. I KNEW NO BETTER THEN.

VERY MUCH.

DO YOU FIND HER MUCH CHANGED, PIP? SHE WAS PROUD AND INSULTING, AND YOU WANTED TO GO AWAY FROM HER.

LESS COARSE AND COMMON?

HA!

THIS IS WHERE YOU GAVE ME MY MEAT[1] AND DRINK.

I DON'T REMEMBER.

NOT REMEMBER THAT YOU MADE ME CRY?

YOU MUST KNOW THAT I HAVE NO HEART – IF THAT HAS ANYTHING TO DO WITH MY MEMORY.

ESTELLA TREATED ME AS A BOY STILL, YET SHE LURED ME ON.

1. MEAT: FOOD (OF ANY KIND).

I THOUGHT I SAW SOME FLEETING RESEMBLANCE IN HER FACE – TO WHOM? I LOOKED AGAIN AND IT WAS GONE.

AS ESTELLA LEFT TO PREPARE FOR DINNER, MISS HAVISHAM DREW MY HEAD CLOSE TO HERS.

LOVE HER! I MADE HER WHAT SHE IS THAT SHE MIGHT BE LOVED. IF SHE TEARS YOUR HEART TO PIECES, LOVE HER!

IT SOUNDED LIKE A CURSE!

I LODGED AT THE BLUE BOAR, THOUGH I KNEW I SHOULD HAVE STAYED WITH JOE.

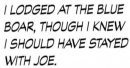

I LOVE HER! I LOVE HER! I LOVE HER!

MISS HAVISHAM MUST MEAN US FOR EACH OTHER!

WHEN I NEXT VISITED OUR TOWN, IT WAS FOR MY SISTER'S FUNERAL. SHE WAS LAID QUIETLY IN THE EARTH, BESIDE OUR PARENTS' GRAVE.

I AM GOING TO TRY TO GET THE PLACE OF MISTRESS[1] AT THE NEW SCHOOL.

HOW ARE YOU GOING TO LIVE, BIDDY?

1. MISTRESS: TEACHER.

OF COURSE, I SHALL BE DOWN HERE OFTEN. I AM NOT GOING TO LEAVE POOR JOE ALONE.

ARE YOU QUITE SURE THAT YOU WILL COME TO SEE HIM OFTEN?

I WAS OFFENDED BY HER DOUBTS, THOUGH I KNEW SHE WAS RIGHT.

NOW, MR. PIP, YOU ARE IN DEBT, OF COURSE?

I AM AFRAID I MUST SAY YES, SIR.

MEANWHILE HERBERT AND I WERE SPENDING LAVISHLY. ON MY TWENTY-FIRST BIRTHDAY, JAGGERS SENT FOR ME.

UNFOLD THIS PIECE OF PAPER AND TELL ME WHAT IT IS.

THIS IS A BANK-NOTE FOR FIVE HUNDRED POUNDS!

AT THE RATE OF THAT HANDSOME SUM PER ANNUM[1] YOU ARE TO LIVE UNTIL THE DONOR[2] OF THE WHOLE APPEARS.

IS MY BENEFACTOR TO BE MADE KNOWN TO ME TODAY?

SHALL I KNOW SOON?

NO. ASK ANOTHER.

THAT'S A QUESTION I MUST NOT BE ASKED. THAT'S ALL I HAVE GOT TO SAY.

1. PER ANNUM: EACH YEAR. 2. DONOR: GIVER.

ESTELLA WAS NOW IN LONDON, BEING INTRODUCED TO THE FASHIONABLE WORLD.

SHE RESENTS ME BECAUSE SHE KNOWS MISS HAVISHAM INTENDS ME FOR HER. SHE FEELS SHE HAS NO CHOICE.

I SAW HER AT PARTIES, OPERAS, CONCERTS, BALLS. HER INDIFFERENCE[1] MADE EACH EVENT A MISERY.

IT MAKES ME WRETCHED THAT YOU ENCOURAGE A MAN LIKE DRUMMLE.

HE HAS NOTHING TO RECOMMEND HIM BUT MONEY.

DON'T BE FOOLISH, PIP. IT'S NOT WORTH DISCUSSING.

YES IT IS. I CANNOT BEAR THAT PEOPLE SHOULD SAY, "SHE THROWS AWAY HER AIRS AND GRACES ON A BOOR,[2] THE LOWEST IN THE CROWD."

SHE HAD COUNTLESS ADMIRERS. BENTLEY DRUMMLE WAS ALWAYS HANGING ABOUT HER.

I CAN BEAR IT.

1 INDIFFERENCE: COMPLETE LACK OF INTEREST. 2. BOOR: BIG, AWKWARD.

I HAVE SEEN YOU GIVE HIM LOOKS AND SMILES SUCH AS YOU NEVER GIVE TO ME.

DO YOU WANT ME THEN TO DECEIVE AND ENTRAP YOU?

DO YOU DECEIVE AND ENTRAP HIM, ESTELLA?

YES, AND MANY OTHERS – ALL OF THEM BUT YOU.

TWO YEARS LATER . . .

THERE IS SOMEONE DOWN THERE, IS THERE NOT? WHAT FLOOR DO YOU WANT?

MR. PIP.

ALONE IN OUR CHAMBERS ON A WILD, WINDY NIGHT, I HEARD FOOTSTEPS ON THE STAIRS.

YOU ACTED NOBLE, MY BOY. NOBLE, PIP! AND I HAVE NEVER FORGOT IT!

IT WAS AN ELDERLY MAN IN A ROUGH COAT, LIKE A SEAFARER. TO MY AMAZEMENT HE HELD OUT HIS ARMS TO ME.

IF YOU HAVE COME TO THANK ME FOR WHAT I DID AS A CHILD, IT WAS NOT NECESSARY.

I KNEW HIM THEN, AFTER ALL THOSE YEARS. IT WAS MY CONVICT!

FEELING I HAD SPOKEN CRUELLY, I OFFERED HIM A DRINK BEFORE HE WENT.

MAY I MAKE SO BOLD AS TO ASK YOU HOW YOU HAVE DONE SO WELL?

I HAVE BEEN CHOSEN TO SUCCEED TO[1] SOME PROPERTY.

MIGHT A MERE WARMINT[2] ASK WHOSE PROPERTY?

I DON'T KNOW.

COULD I MAKE A GUESS AT YOUR INCOME SINCE YOU COME OF AGE? THE FIRST FIGURE NOW. FIVE?

CONCERNING A GUARDIAN.[3] SOME LAWYER, MAYBE. THE FIRST LETTER OF HIS NAME, NOW. WOULD IT BE J?

ESTELLA! ESTELLA! MISS HAVISHAM'S INTENTIONS – ALL A DREAM!

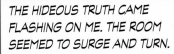

THE HIDEOUS TRUTH CAME FLASHING ON ME. THE ROOM SEEMED TO SURGE AND TURN.

1. SUCCEED TO: INHERIT. 2. WARMINT: AN UNDESIRABLE PERSON (A VARIANT OF "VERMIN").
3. GUARDIAN: A PERSON WHO TAKES THE PLACE OF A PARENT FOR A YOUNG PERSON WHOSE PARENTS ARE DEAD.

SO THIS WAS MY FAIRY GODMOTHER! A CRIMINAL, AN OUTCAST, GUILTY PERHAPS OF TERRIBLE CRIMES.

YES, DEAR BOY, IT'S ME WOT HAS DONE IT!

THAT DUNGHILL DOG WOT YOU KEP' LIFE IN GOT HIS HEAD SO HIGH THAT HE COULD MAKE YOU A GENTLEMAN.

I COULD NOT HAVE FEARED AND LOATHED HIM MORE IF HE HAD BEEN A WILD BEAST.

I'M YOUR SECOND FATHER, PIP. I'VE PUT AWAY MONEY IN AUSTRALIA,[1] ONLY FOR YOU TO SPEND, AND I'VE HELD STEADY IN MY MIND TO COME ONE DAY AND SEE MY BOY.

SO IT WAS FOR THIS WRETCH AND HIS FILTHY MONEY THAT I ABANDONED JOE!

HOW LONG? I'M NO A-GOING BACK. I'V COME FOR GOOD

MIND YOU, CAUTION IS NECESSARY. I WAS SENT FOR LIFE. IT'S DEATH[2] TO COME BACK.

HOW LONG DO YOU REMAIN?

THIS WAS ALL I NEEDED. THE MAN WAS RISKING HIS LIFE FOR ME! I FELT I HAD A DUTY TO PROTECT HIM.

1. AUSTRALIA: THE CONVICT HAS BEEN TRANSPORTED (SENT AS PUNISHMENT) TO AUSTRALIA. 2. DEATH: UNDER ENGLISH LAW, A CRIMINAL TRANSPORTED TO AUSTRALIA FOR LIFE FACED THE DEATH PENALTY IF HE RETURNED.

WHERE ARE YOU TO LIVE? WHERE WILL YOU BE SAFE?

THE DANGER AIN'T SO GREAT. WHO KNOWS ME HERE? THERE'S WEMMICK AND THERE'S JAGGERS AND THERE'S YOU. WHO ELSE IS TO INFORM?

THERE IS NO PERSON WHO MIGHT IDENTIFY YOU IN THE STREET?

NO-ONE BAR[3] COMPEYSON. AND NO REASON TO THINK HE'S IN LONDON.

I FOUND ROOMS FOR HIM NEARBY AND GOT HIM SOME DECENT CLOTHES – THOUGH HIS PAST LIFE GAVE HIM A SAVAGE AIR NO CLOTHES COULD TAME.

THAT'S IT, DEAR BOY, CALL ME UNCLE. THOUGH MY NAME IS MAGWITCH, CHRISTENED ABEL.

I DO NOT KNOW WHAT NAME TO CALL YOU. I HAVE GIVEN OUT[4] YOU ARE MY UNCLE.

3. BAR: EXCEPT.
4. GIVEN OUT: TOLD PEOPLE.

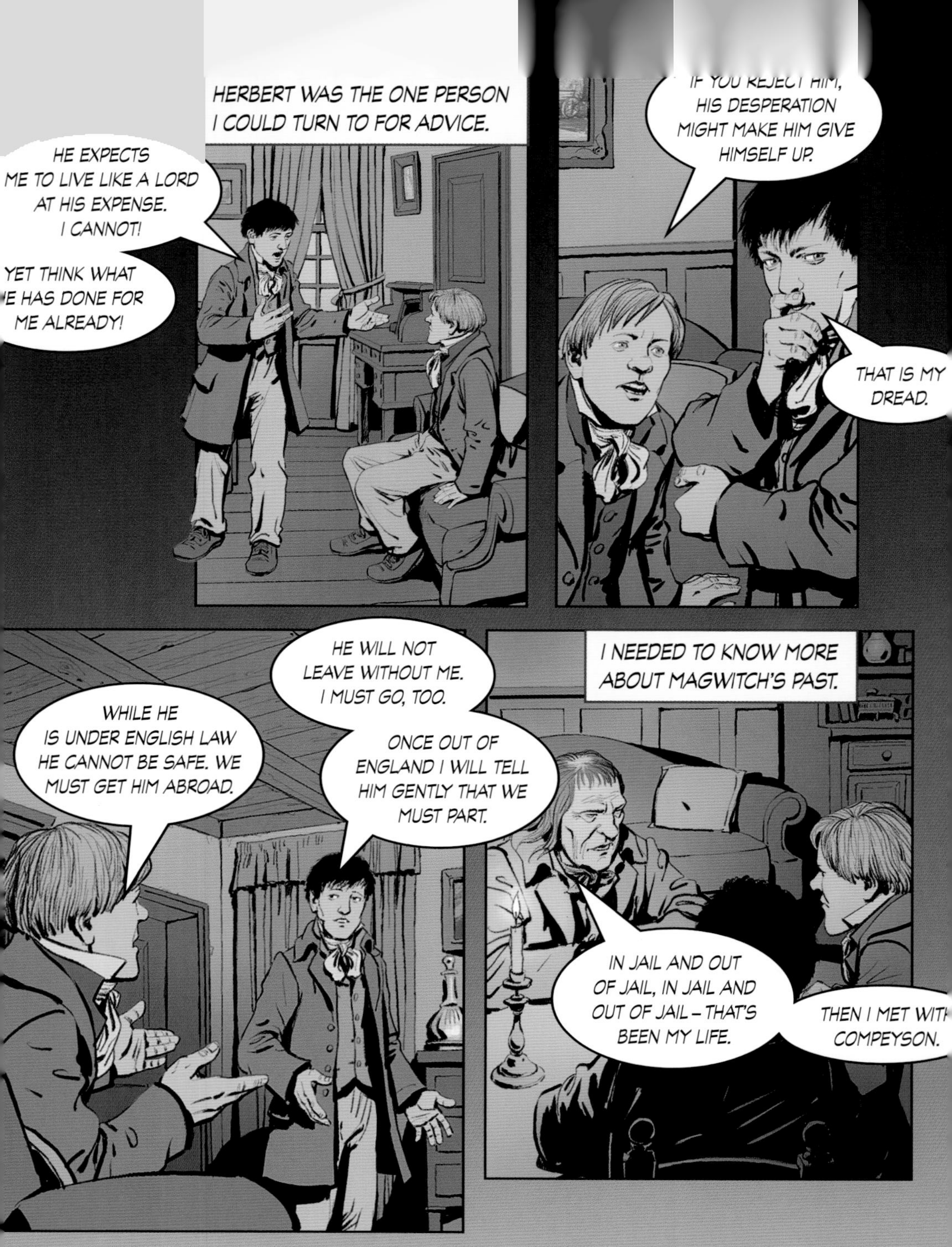
HERBERT WAS THE ONE PERSON I COULD TURN TO FOR ADVICE.
HE EXPECTS ME TO LIVE LIKE A LORD AT HIS EXPENSE. I CANNOT!
YET THINK WHAT HE HAS DONE FOR ME ALREADY!
IF YOU REJECT HIM, HIS DESPERATION MIGHT MAKE HIM GIVE HIMSELF UP.
THAT IS MY DREAD.
WHILE HE IS UNDER ENGLISH LAW HE CANNOT BE SAFE. WE MUST GET HIM ABROAD.
HE WILL NOT LEAVE WITHOUT ME. I MUST GO, TOO.
ONCE OUT OF ENGLAND I WILL TELL HIM GENTLY THAT WE MUST PART.
I NEEDED TO KNOW MORE ABOUT MAGWITCH'S PAST.
IN JAIL AND OUT OF JAIL, IN JAIL AND OUT OF JAIL – THAT'S BEEN MY LIFE.
THEN I MET WITH COMPEYSON.

HE SET UP FUR A GENTLEMAN, THIS COMPEYSON. TOOK ME ON AS PARDNER[1] AND MADE ME HIS SLAVE.

WHAT WAS HIS BUSINESS?

SWINDLING, FORGERY AND SUCHLIKE. HE'D NO MORE HEART THAN AN IRON FILE AND WAS AS COLD AS DEATH.

WE WERE TOOK[2] AND TRIED TOGETHER, BUT WHEN EVIDENCE WAS GIV', IT WAS ALWAYS ME THAT SEEMED TO HAVE WORKED THE THING[3] AND GOT THE PROFIT.

COMPEYSON GOT OFF LIGHTLY FOR HIS GOOD CHARACTER, BEING KNOWN TO WITNESSES IN HIGH SOCIETY –

– AND WARN'T IT ME WAS PUT IN IRONS AND SENT TO AUSTRALIA?

HERBERT PASSED ME A NOTE HE HAD WRITTEN ON THE COVER OF A BOOK.

'COMPEYSON IS THE MAN WHO PROFESSED[4] TO BE MISS HAVISHAM'S LOVER.'

1. PARDNER: BUSINESS PARTNER. 2. TOOK: ARRESTED.
3. WORKED THE THING: COMMITTED THE CRIME.
4. PROFESSED: PRETENDED.

47

WE HAD TO LEAVE ENGLAND BEFORE COMPEYSON INFORMED ON MAGWITCH. BUT FIRST I MUST SEE ESTELLA ONE LAST TIME.

MISS HAVISHAM, I AM AS UNHAPPY AS YOU EVER CAN HAVE MEANT ME TO BE.

I HAVE FOUND OUT WHO MY PATRON[1] IS. IT WAS NOT A FORTUNATE DISCOVERY. IT SEEMS I CAME TO YOU ONLY TO GRATIFY A WHIM.[2]

AY, PIP, YOU DID.

AND THAT MR. JAGGERS—

MR. JAGGERS HAD NOTHING TO DO WITH IT. HIS BEING MY LAWYER IS A COINCIDENCE.

YOU MADE YOUR OWN SNARES.[3] I NEVER MADE THEM.

BUT YOU LET ME GO ON IN THEM. WAS THAT KIND?

WHO AM I, FOR GOD'S SAKE, THAT I SHOULD BE KIND?

1. PATRON: SUPPORTER, PROVIDER. 2. ONLY TO GRATIFY A WHIM: ONLY BECAUSE YOU FELT LIKE IT.
3. SNARES: TRAPS. SHE MEANS THAT HE ALLOWED HIMSELF TO BE TAKEN IN BY HIS OWN IMAGIINATION.

ESTELLA, YOU KNOW I LOVE YOU – THAT HAVE LOVED YOU LONG AND DEARLY.

DRUMMLE ALWAYS AT YOUR SIDE. BUT YOU WOULD NEVER MARRY HIM?

I KNOW LOVE ONLY AS A FORM OF WORDS, NOT IN MY BREAST. I HAVE TRIED TO WARN YOU OF THIS.

BETTER HIM THAN A MAN WHO WOULD REALIZE I TOOK NOTHING TO HIM.[1]

WHY NOT TELL THE TRUTH? I AM GOING TO MARRY HIM.

IT WAS PAST MIDNIGHT WHEN I REACHED OUR CHAMBERS. THE NIGHT PORTER HANDED ME A NOTE IN WEMMICK'S WRITING.

"DON'T GO HOME."

..TOOK NOTHING TO HIM: HAD NOTHING TO OFFER HIM.

NOW, PIP, BE CAREFUL. DON'T TELL ME ANYTHING. I DON'T WANT TO KNOW.

MR. JAGGERS WAS DETERMINED NOT TO GET INVOLVED.

I DREW WEMMICK ASIDE TO SPEAK MORE FREELY.

I HEARD THAT YOUR CHAMBERS HAD BEEN WATCHED.

WOULD IT BE RELATED TO A PERSON CALLED COMPEYSON?

WEMMICK SEEMED TO NOD.

I TOLD MR. HERBERT THAT IF HE KNEW OF ANY TOM, JACK OR RICHARD[1] LODGING NEAR YOU HE HAD BETTER GET HIM OUT OF THE WAY QUICK.

MR. HERBERT HAS FOUND A PLACE FOR HIM DOWN BY THE POOL.[2]

1. ANY TOM, JACK OR RICHARD: SOMEONE OR OTHER. (THE MODERN PHRASE IS "TOM, DICK OR HARRY.") 2. THE POOL: THE POOL OF LONDON–THE STRETCH OF THE RIVER THAMES FROM LONDON BRIDGE TO ROTHERHITHE IN SOUTHEAST LONDON. THE POOL WAS THE ORIGINAL PORT OF LONDON.

NOW THAT'S A GOOD SPOT FOR THREE REASONS. FIRST: IN CASE OF YOUR BEING FOLLOWED, IT'S OUT OF YOUR BEAT.[1]

SECOND: MR. HERBERT KNOWS THE LANDLADY, SO WITHOUT GOING NEAR IT YOURSELF YOU CAN HEAR OF THE SAFETY OF TOM, JACK OR RICHARD THROUGH HIM.

THIRDLY: IF YOU WANT TO SLIP TOM, JACK OR RICHARD ON BOARD A FOREIGN PACKET-BOAT,[2] THERE HE IS – BY THE RIVER – READY.

AFTER DARK I WENT TO THE HOUSE BY THE RIVER TO TELL MAGWITCH ABOUT WEMMICK'S PLAN. HIS MANNER SEEMED GENTLER. I NO LONGER SHRANK FROM HIM.

WHEN THE TIME COMES I WILL GO WITH YOU.

I'VE LITTLE FEAR OF MY SAFETY WITH SUCH GOOD HELP, DEAR BOY.

1. OUT OF YOUR BEAT: FAR AWAY FROM THE PLACES YOU USUALLY GO TO.
2. PACKET-BOAT: A BOAT CARRYING GOODS, PASSENGERS AND MAIL TO A REGULAR TIMETABLE.

MR. JAGGERS ASKED ME AND WEMMICK TO DINE.

SO HERE'S TO MRS. BENTLEY DRUMMLE. YOU'VE HEARD OF HER MARRIAGE, PIP?

BEFORE I COULD ANSWER, THE HOUSEKEEPER CAME IN. FOR THE FIRST TIME I SAW DIRECTLY INTO HER FACE.

THOSE EYES—I COULD NEVER MISTAKE THEM!

AND THAT LOOK, SO INTENT!

MR. JAGGERS WAS IMPATIENT WITH HER. SHE TWITCHED HER FINGERS NERVOUSLY, AS IF SHE WERE KNITTING.

MOLLY, HOW SLOW YOU ARE TODAY!

ESTELLA'S HANDS! ESTELLA'S FACE—AS YEARS OF BRUTAL LIVING WOULD SHAPE IT.

THAT IS ESTELLA'S MOTHER!

LATER I ASKED WEMMICK TO TELL ME MORE ABOUT THE HOUSEKEEPER.

TWENTY YEARS AGO THAT WOMAN FACED A MURDER CHARGE—STRANGLING ANOTHER WOMAN—CASE OF JEALOUSY.

MR. JAGGERS GOT HER OFF. MANAGED TO ARGUE SHE HADN'T THE STRENGTH TO DO IT. SHE HAS BEEN IN HIS SERVICE EVER SINCE.

THE PROSECUTION CLAIMED SHE'D KILLED HER CHILD BY THIS MAN THEY FOUGHT OVER, TO REVENGE HERSELF ON HIM.

HOW OLD WAS THE CHILD – WHAT SEX?

SOME THREE YEARS OLD. SAID TO HAVE BEEN A GIRL.

MR. JAGGERS HAD TOLD ME MISS HAVISHAM WAS ANXIOUS TO SEE ME.

PERHAPS YOU CAN NEVER BELIEVE NOW THAT THERE IS ANYTHING HUMAN IN MY HEART?

IF YOU CAN EVER BRING YOURSELF TO SAY "I FORGIVE HER," PRAY DO IT.

I CAN DO IT NOW. I WANT FORGIVENESS FAR TOO MUCH TO BE BITTER WITH YOU.

OH, WHAT HAVE I DONE? I STOLE HER HEART AWAY AND PUT ICE IN ITS PLACE.

IF YOU CAN UNDO A SCRAP OF WHAT YOU HAVE DONE IN WARPING ESTELLA'S NATURE[1] –

PIP, BELIEVE ME, I MEANT TO SAVE HER FROM MISERY LIKE MINE.[2]

1. WARPING ESTELLA'S NATURE: CHANGING HER CHARACTER FOR THE WORSE.
2. MISERY LIKE MINE: BECAUSE MISS HAVISHAM WAS HURT BY THE MAN SHE LOVED, SHE THOUGHT SHE COULD SAVE ESTELLA BY TEACHING HER NEVER TO LOVE ANYONE.

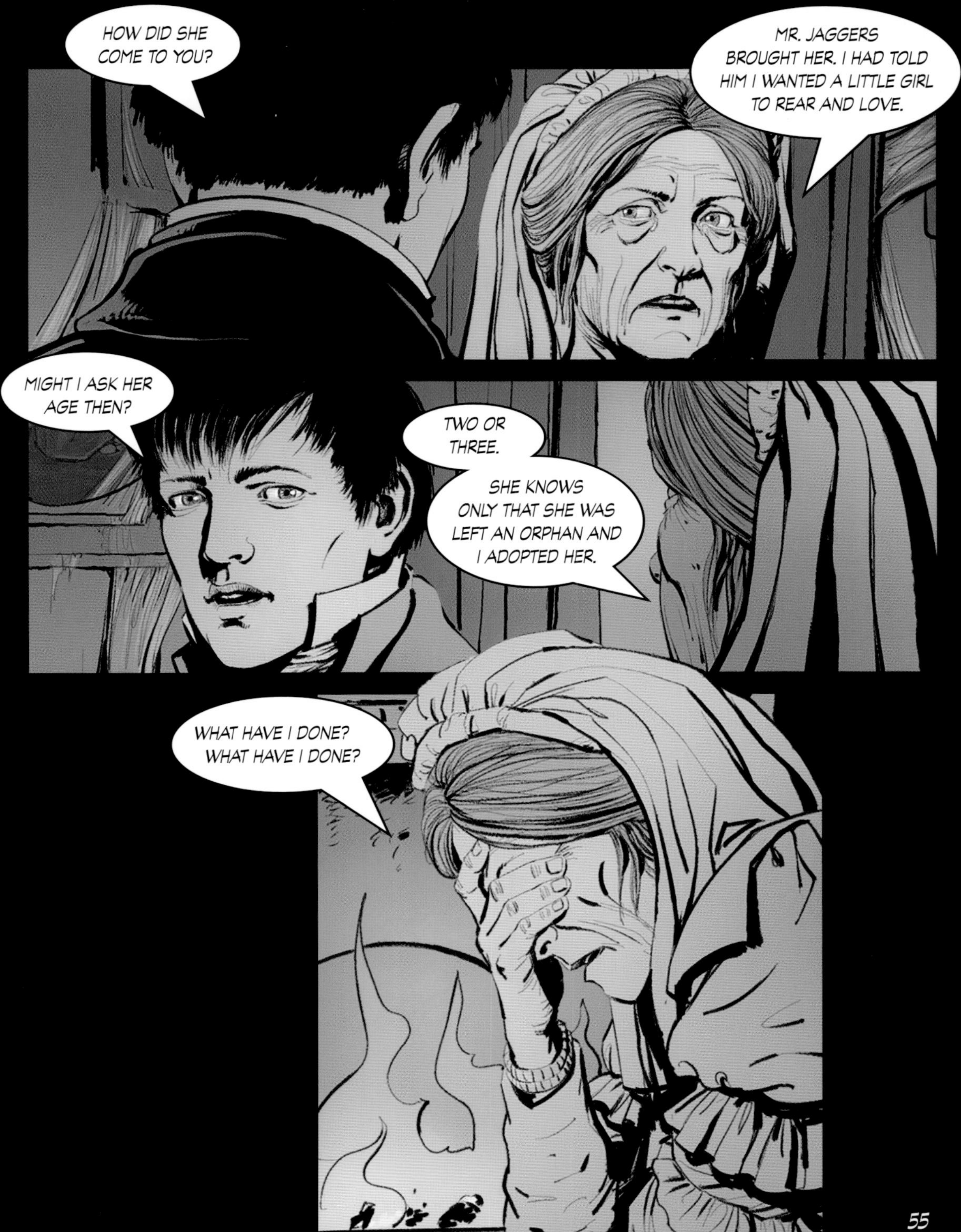
HOW DID SHE COME TO YOU?
MR. JAGGERS BROUGHT HER. I HAD TOLD HIM I WANTED A LITTLE GIRL TO REAR AND LOVE.
MIGHT I ASK HER AGE THEN?
TWO OR THREE.
SHE KNOWS ONLY THAT SHE WAS LEFT AN ORPHAN AND I ADOPTED HER.
WHAT HAVE I DONE? WHAT HAVE I DONE?

AS I WAS LEAVING, A COAL MUST HAVE FALLEN FROM THE FIRE.

AAAAAH!

MY GOD!

WE STRUGGLED LIKE DESPERATE ENEMIES—

—I TRYING TO WRAP HER, SHE WILDLY SHRIEKING AND TRYING TO FREE HERSELF.

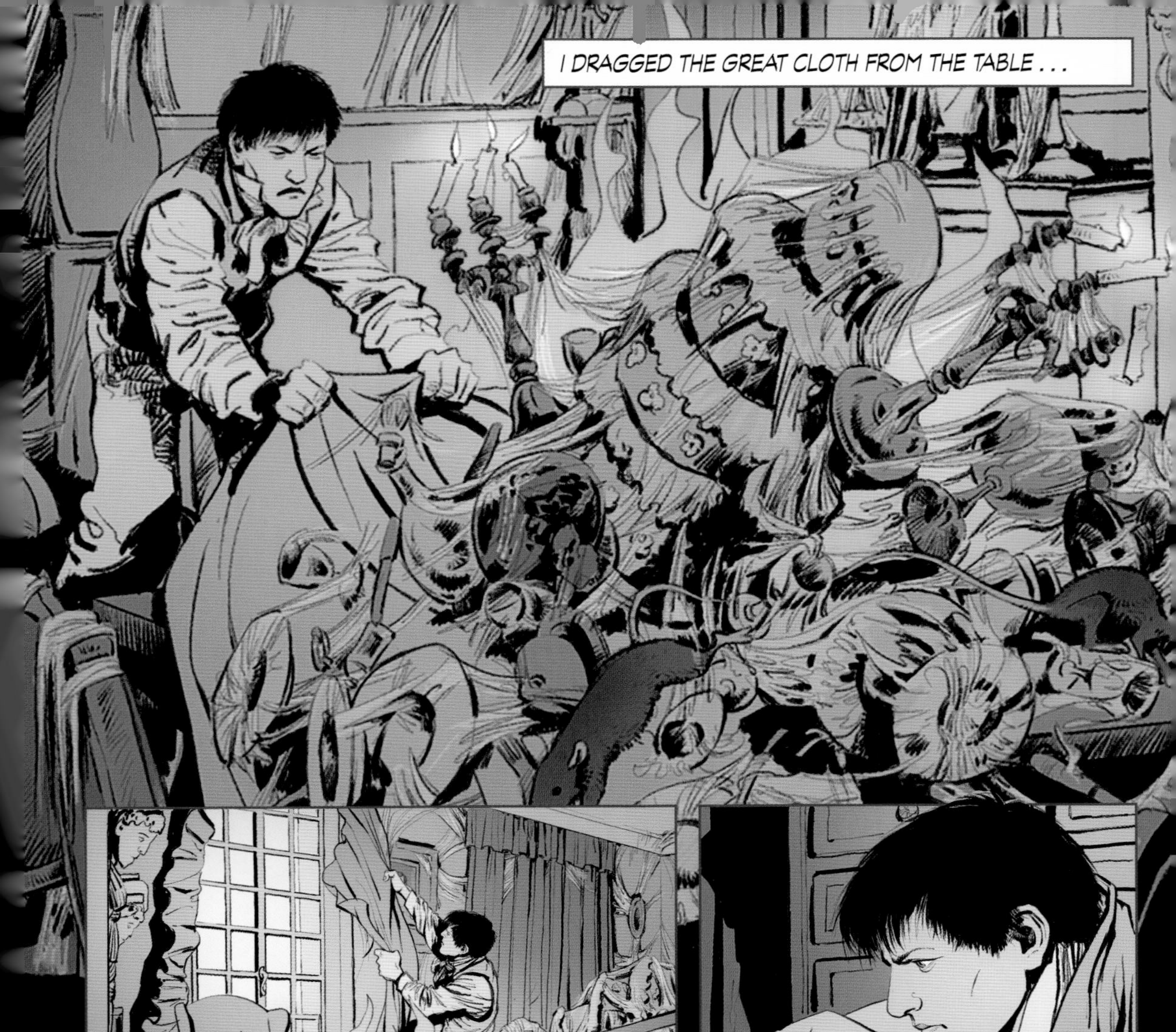
I DRAGGED THE GREAT CLOTH FROM THE TABLE . . .
. . . AND THE CURTAINS FROM THE WINDOWS.

A GOOD TWO HOURS. HE IMPROVES.

HE IS NOT A BAD MAN. HE HAS HAD A WRETCHED LIFE.

MY HANDS AND ARMS WERE BADLY BURNED.

TO THE LAST DEGREE.

THEY HAD A CHILD OF WHOM MAGWITCH WAS EXCEEDINGLY FOND, BUT IT SEEMS SHE KILLED IT.

HE COULD NEVER TRACE EITHER OF THEM.

"BURN AS SOON AS READ. ON WEDNESDAY YOU MIGHT DO WHAT YOU KNOW OF. NOW BURN."

HERBERT, I AM NOT FEVERISH, AM I? MY MIND IS NOT WANDERING?

I BELIEVE THE MAN WE HAVE IN HIDING DOWN THE RIVER IS ESTELLA'S FATHER.

AT LAST THE NEWS CAME THAT THE COAST WAS CLEAR.

WE PLANNED TO ROW MAGWITCH AS FAR DOWN RIVER AS POSSIBLE BEFORE NIGHTFALL.

BEYOND GRAVESEND, THE PACKET-BOAT IS NOT LIKELY TO BE SEARCHED.

WE WOULD STAY OVERNIGHT AND HAIL A FOREIGN VESSEL

WHAT WAS THAT RIPPLE?

IS THAT A BOAT YONDER?

WE STOPPED AT A LONELY INN.

THEY COULD BE CUSTOMS MEN LOOKING FOR SMUGGLERS.

BY NIGHTFALL WE WERE IN THE SOLITARY REACHES OF THE THAMES BETWEEN ESSEX AND KENT. THE FEAR THAT WE WERE SUSPECTED OR FOLLOWED WAS ALWAYS IN OUR MINDS.

WOKEN IN THE NIGHT BY THE CREAKING INN SIGN, I SAW TWO MEN PEERING INTO OUR BOAT.

THERE WAS NO SIGN OF THEM NEXT DAY AS WE ROWED OUT TO MEET THE HAMBURG[1] STEAMER.

BUT SUDDENLY A BOAT SHOT OUT FROM THE BANK AND DREW ALONGSIDE US.

I CALL UPON HIM TO SURRENDER, AND YOU TO ASSIST.

YOU HAVE A RETURNED TRANSPORT[2] THERE, NAME OF ABEL MAGWITCH.

STOP THE PADDLES!

COMPEYSON!

THE STEAMER WAS ALMOST UPON US WHEN MAGWITCH FLUNG HIMSELF AT ONE OF THE PASSENGERS IN THE OTHER BOAT.

HAMBURG: A MAJOR PORT IN NORTHERN GERMANY. 2. TRANSPORT: A CONVICT WHO HAS BEEN TRANSPORTED TO AUSTRALIA.

MAGWITCH WAS SEVERELY INJURED.

WE WENT DOWN TOGETHER AND FOUGHT UNDER WATER.

I CAN'T SAY WHAT I MAY HAVE DONE TO HIM, BUT I BROKE FREE.

COMPEYSON'S BODY WAS FOUND LATER.

I FELT THE STEAMER'S IMPACT AS THE BOAT SANK BENEATH ME. HERBERT AND I WERE HAULED ABOARD THE POLICE BOAT.

I KNEW THERE WAS NO HOPE THAT MAGWITCH WOULD BE SPARED THE DEATH PENALTY. TO THINK THAT HE HAD COME HOME FOR MY SAKE!

HOW MUCH BETTER A MAN HE IS THAN I HAVE BEEN TO JOE.

DEAR BOY, I'M QUITE CONTENT TO TAKE MY CHANCE. I'VE SEEN MY BOY, AND HE CAN BE A GENTLEMAN WITHOUT ME.

WHILE MAGWITCH AWAITED TRIAL, HERBERT TOLD ME HE MUST LEAVE ENGLAND SOON.

THE FIRM IS SENDING ME TO CAIRO.[1] WOULD YOU CONSIDER WORKING WITH ME THERE?

IF YOU THOUGHT YOU COULD LEAVE THE OFFER OPEN FOR A WHILE . . .

FOR A LITTLE WHILE – SIX MONTHS, A YEAR.

TWO OR THREE MONTHS AT MOST!

1. CAIRO: THE CAPITAL OF EGYPT. THE ENGLISH FIRM THAT HERBERT WORKS FOR HAS ITS OWN OFFICE THERE.

BY THE TIME OF HIS TRIAL MAGWITCH WAS VERY ILL.

GOD BLESS YOU. YOU'VE NEVER DESERTED ME, DEAR BOY.

I MEANT TO, AT FIRST. HOW LITTLE I DESERVE HIS FAITH IN ME.

YOU KNEW THE PENALTY OF RETURNING. YOU RETURNED. THE SENTENCE MUST BE DEATH.

MY LORD, I HAVE RECEIVED MY SENTENCE OF DEATH FROM THE ALMIGHTY,[1] BUT I BOW TO YOURS.

I NOW PRAYED THAT HE MIGHT DIE BEFORE THE DAY OF EXECUTION.

ON MY NEXT VISIT I SAW A GREAT CHANGE IN HIM. HE LAY CALMLY LOOKING AT THE CEILING.

HE SMILED.

O LORD, BE MERCIFUL TO HIM, A SINNER.[2]

DEAR MAGWITCH, YOU HAD A CHILD WHOM YOU LOVED AND LOST.

THEN HIS HEAD DROPPED QUIETLY ONTO HIS BREAST.

SHE IS LIVING, SHE IS A LADY AND VERY BEAUTIFUL, AND I LOVE HER.

1. THE ALMIGHTY: GOD. MAGWITCH KNOWS THAT HE IS ALREADY DYING FROM HIS INJURIES. 2. O LORD . . . : PIP IS QUOTING FROM THE BIBLE, LUKE 13:18.

61

AT LAST I MADE A DECISION: I WOULD GO BACK TO WORK IN THE FORGE AND MARRY BIDDY – IF SHE WOULD FORGIVE MY FAULTS. BUT I WAS TOO LATE!

DEAR BIDDY, HOW SMART YOU ARE! AND JOE, HOW SMART YOU ARE!

IT IS MY WEDDING DAY AND I AM MARRIED TO JOE!

BIDDY, YOU HAVE THE BEST HUSBAND IN THE WHOLE WORLD.

I SOLD ALL I HAD[1] AND JOINED HERBERT IN CAIRO. HOW COULD I EVER HAVE THOUGHT HE WOULD NOT SUCCEED IN BUSINESS? I WAS THE ONE WHO LACKED JUDGEMENT.

IT WAS ELEVEN YEARS BEFORE I COULD VISIT BIDDY AND JOE.

WE GIV' HIM THE NAME OF PIP FOR YOUR SAKE.

YOU MUST MARRY, TOO, PIP, AND HAVE A SON.

THE CHILD SEATED BY THE FIRE WAS LIKE MY YOUNGER SELF.

WE SPOKE OF ESTELLA. HER BRUTAL HUSBAND WAS DEAD.

ARE YOU SURE YOU DON'T STILL FRET FOR HER, PIP?

THAT POOR DREAM HAS ALL GONE BY, BIDDY.

1. I SOLD ALL I HAD: PIP IS NO LONGER RICH. WHEN MAGWITCH WAS CONDEMNED TO DEATH, ALL HIS MONEY WAS CONFISCATED BY THE CROWN.

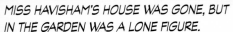
MISS HAVISHAM'S HOUSE WAS GONE, BUT IN THE GARDEN WAS A LONE FIGURE.

ESTELLA!

I CAME TO TAKE LEAVE OF THE POOR OLD PLACE BEFORE IT WAS BUILT OVER.

I HAVE OFTEN THOUGHT OF YOU – VERY OFTEN.

YOU HAVE ALWAYS HELD YOUR PLACE IN MY HEART.

SUFFERING HAS TAUGHT ME HOW YOUR HEART ONCE SUFFERED.

I HAVE BEEN BENT AND BROKEN – I THINK, INTO A BETTER SHAPE.

BE GOOD TO ME AND TELL ME WE ARE FRIENDS.

WE ARE FRIENDS.

AND WILL CONTINUE TO BE FRIENDS APART.

AS WE LEFT THAT RUINED PLACE TOGETHER, I SAW NO SHADOW OF ANOTHER PARTING.[1]

1. NO SHADOW OF ANOTHER PARTING: NO DANGER THAT WE WOULD PART AGAIN.

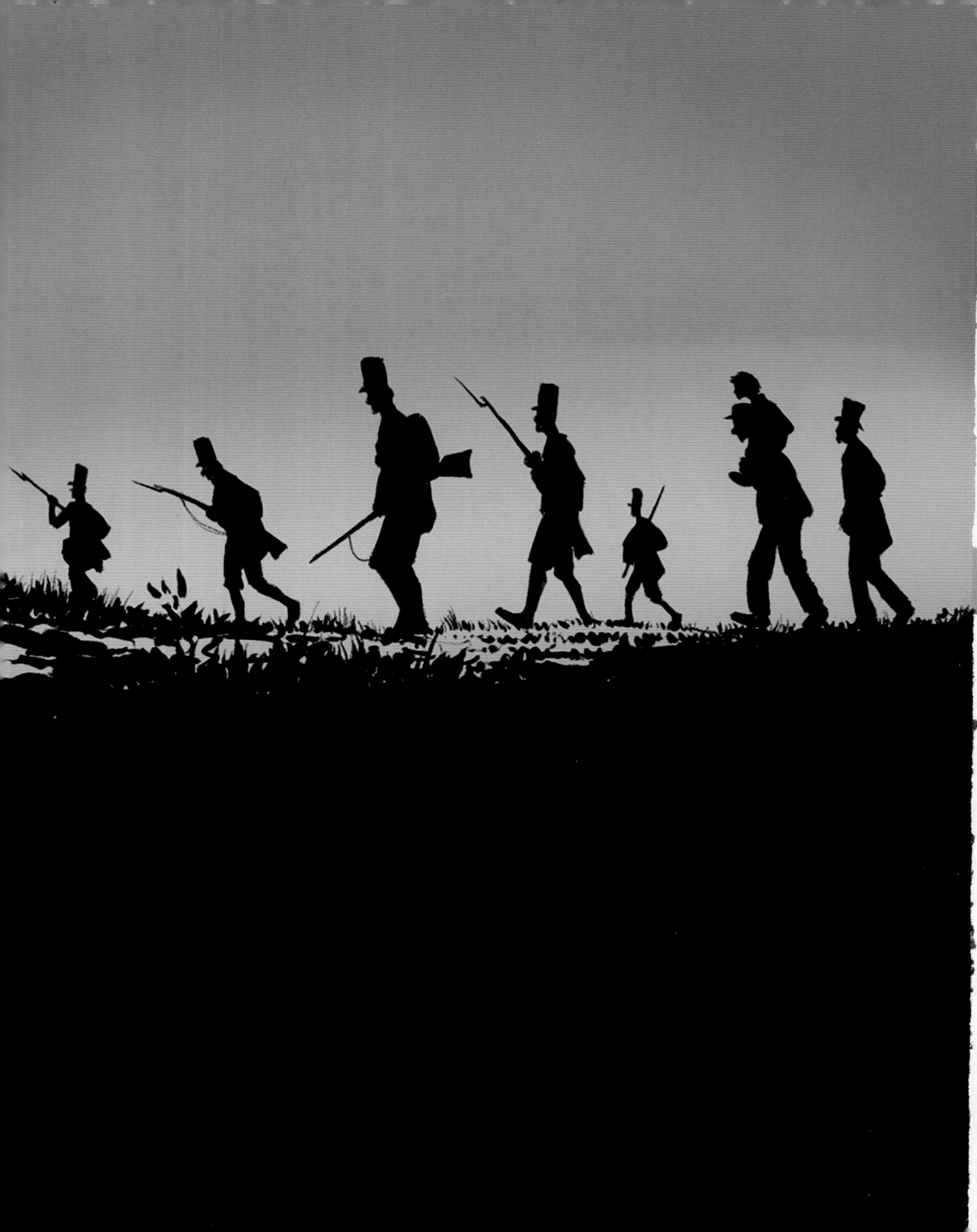